"Joshua, what did you do or say to someone in the Bureau to get you shunted over here?"

Joshua felt his cheeks flush. "You don't want to know," he told her, meaning every word of it. He had no desire to tell Kyra all the stupid choices he'd made in the last eight months. He was probably lucky that the worst his actions had earned him was this dead-end investigator's assignment. If this was the answer to that prayer—or whatever it had been—in his car a few days ago, it was a pretty goofy answer. "So fill me in on what we've got so far. Nobody at the Bureau seemed to have a lot of information.'

"That's because there isn't much yet," she said. "I can let you have a corner of my office to use for your research."

"Great," he said weakly. Maybe this assignment would teach him to improve his attitude. A few weeks of working closely with Kyra would either reform him or send him over the edge.

Books by Lynn Bulock

Love Inspired Suspense

Where Truth Lies #56
No Love Lost #59
To Trust a Stranger #69
To Trust a Friend #108

Love Inspired

Gifts of Grace #80
Looking for Miracles #97
Walls of Jericho #125
The Prodigal's Return #144
Change of the Heart #181
The Harbor of His Arms #204
Protecting Holly #279

Steeple Hill Single Title

Love the Sinner
Less Than Frank

LYNN BULOCK

lives in Thousand Oaks, California, with her husband of nearly thirty years. They have two grown sons. When she's not writing, Lynn stays active in many ministries of her church, including serving as a Stephen Ministry Leader.

Lynn Bulock

to
TRUST a FRIEND

Steeple Hill®

Published by Steeple Hill Books™

STEEPLE HILL BOOKS

Steeple
Hill®

ISBN-13: 978-0-373-44298-0
ISBN-10:   0-373-44298-X

TO TRUST A FRIEND

Copyright © 2008 by Lynn M. Bulock

Printed in U.S.A.

And those who know your name put their trust in you; for you, O Lord, have not forsaken those who seek you.

—*Psalms* 9:10

To Joe, always

Soli Deo Gloria

PROLOGUE

Would he be eternally condemned for breaking his promise? The Watcher stood in a clump of trees that hid him from the two old people with binoculars and pondered the question. It wasn't as if it had been a promise to God, but it had been a promise to Mama and she'd asked him to promise before God. He'd kept his promise while she was alive, but she was dead now and he could hardly contain himself.

For six long years he'd been good. He'd gone to work every day, kept to himself, hadn't strayed into those places that called to him and drew him toward the Bad Things. But Mama had died years ago and the pull of his promise was weakening. The voices had stopped whispering in his ear and were speaking out loud. The little girls had started staring at him again, almost begging him to take action. Before long he wouldn't be able to control the voices any more. Promise or no promise, he was going to have to start hunting again. Soon.

For a long time just visiting here had been enough.

Then, this year's heavy spring rains had overrun the tiny creek, making it into a regular stream. The whole area had turned into a marshy mess, changing his special place so that he could hardly recognize it.

Nothing was in the right place. Things he'd hidden sat out in the open. His treasures lay strewn about, displayed for anybody to see. That was not a good thing. And now, when he needed to be alone, these two gray-haired old fools were here and they wouldn't leave. They'd stayed in a twenty-foot-square area for more than an hour now, whispering to each other once in a while, pointing to something up in one of the trees.

Suddenly one of them gasped, making the Watcher jump. He cursed silently as a twig snapped under his feet, but nobody noticed except maybe a bird that flew out of the treetops.

"Helen, don't move," the old man said to his companion. "Does your cell phone get any reception out here?"

"Why, Roy? What's going on?" The old lady's voice quavered.

"I found something I think the police are going to want to see," Roy said.

"It's not…a body, is it?" Helen's voice shook.

Roy was silent for a minute. "Not exactly. It was a body once, or at least part of one. What it is now is a very small pile of bones. I can't even tell for sure if they're human or not."

Helen sighed with what sounded like relief. "Just bones? Then it's probably something a dog killed and dragged under here."

"I don't think so. Do you have a signal?"

"Just a minute, Roy." The Watcher could hear the faint short tune of a phone being turned on. "Now it's on. I don't get the best reception out here, but it looks like I could make a call."

"Good. Then dial 911." Roy's voice sounded firm.

"That number is for emergencies, Roy. I don't see what the emergency is here. It's not like anything is going to move."

"Just dial 911, Helen. The police are going to want to see this before anybody gets a chance to mess it all up."

"All right." While Helen talked to the dispatcher, the Watcher realized that it was time to get out of here. Being here when the police arrived would be a major problem. Then he would be condemned for sure, and much sooner than he wanted to think about.

ONE

Just once, Kyra thought, *it would be nice to be treated like a lady.* In old movies and books, heroes were always holding up their hands and saying, "Please, there are ladies present" when people got out of hand. She wondered if anybody would ever treat her that way. Maybe this wish was a little over the top— because Kyra Elliott didn't see herself as the ladylike type—but being treated like something other than one of the boys would be good.

It wasn't as if she looked like one of the boys. She wore her dark auburn hair long, sometimes restraining the waves while she worked, but still in a feminine style. Her clothes were not terribly girlie and were often covered by a lab coat or evidence coveralls, but no one would have mistaken her for anything but a woman.

Still, there was something about her that always seemed to make the men she worked with treat her as if she was just one of the crew. Sometimes there were advantages to that, she decided as she watched her colleagues from the lab continue their mild harassment of a Maryland state trooper. At least they were honest and open around her. They didn't try to hide their shenanigans, either.

While Bill and Terry pointed out all the more spectacular things about the contents of the body bag that the young man had brought in, Kyra stood nearby. The trooper, who must have been all of twenty-two, tried not to lose it in front of the two older, more seasoned men. He wasn't doing all that well, turning a pale shade of green under his tanned skin and short blond hair. After a few minutes Kyra knew it was time to step in.

"Come on, guys, knock it off," she finally said. "Don't let them get to you," Kyra told the young officer. "They only give you a hard time because all of this bothers them, too."

"Come on, Doc, we were only having a little fun," Terry grumbled. The older of the two technicians, he should have known better. The trooper probably wasn't much older than the son Kyra had seen in pictures on Terry's desk.

"Well, save it for a more appropriate time," she told them, watching relief wash over the trooper's face. "Right now we need to get a report from this man so that he can be on his way." She looked pointedly at Bill, who nodded curtly and picked up one of their handheld computer units to check everything in. Kyra stood nearby without comment until she was sure that the lab workers were back on track doing their job properly, then she stepped away to continue her paperwork. Even the advances of modern technology hadn't eliminated all of the forms and irritations of her job. While a lot could be done on computers, there were still papers the state crime lab insisted on using.

"You're still not used to them," Allie said quietly, looking over to the technicians. Kyra's assistant was so astute that she often forgot that Allie was about the same age as the young trooper. In the two months Kyra had been on this job she'd proved invaluable.

Kyra sighed softly. "You're right. Things were a lot different at the university. It was quiet there, and everybody was respectful of the work we did."

"Do you regret coming over here?" Allie peered over the top of her gold wire glasses, which slipped down the soft bridge of her nose.

"Not really. I know this is where I belong. The criminal consulting work we did in my department there was what made me come alive." When the state of Maryland approached her with an offer to lead a forensic anthropology group in their newly expanded state crime lab, Kyra had few doubts about taking the job. And the ease of her transition from the university had only reinforced her feeling that the change was part of God's plan for her life right now. But there were still a few times like today when she missed the quieter atmosphere in academic research. She had to admit, it wasn't always peaceful at the university; lab workers seemed to know who was the most squeamish and capitalized on that for fun there, too. But it hadn't happened as often or as rowdily.

Sighing again, Kyra watched her team members

take the trooper's report and shake his hand in a friendly manner. She knew that Terry and Bill meant well; they had just been at their jobs so long that death didn't bother them very much anymore. It surprised them when outsiders were disturbed by the environment in the labs, and they tended to harp on that feeling. How could she find a way to change their way of reacting without calling them to task too hard? Both of her lab techs were basically good people and Kyra wanted to bring that out in them.

Before she could puzzle that through any further, Allie touched her arm lightly, making Kyra jump. "Sorry, Dr. Elliott. I didn't mean to startle you. But you've got a call on line one and it sounds urgent."

Kyra nodded and went searching for the phone. Fortunately, the handset had actually been set in its cradle on the corner of a countertop instead of being put down someplace under a pile of papers.

"Kyra Elliott." She made another mental note to talk to Allie about calling her by her formal title. Unless there were higher-ups from the crime labs present, Kyra thought titles were pretty stuffy.

The person on the other end identified himself as a detective sergeant with the state police, and any hopes Kyra had of an uneventful day catching up on paperwork went right out the window. "We've got something out here you have to see," the man said, a grim set to his voice. "You'll need a crew." He gave her directions to a spot Kyra knew to be the overgrown edges of a state park where recent floods had made things inaccessible for a couple of weeks. Now the water had receded, replaced by late-spring sunshine. The commander's tone told her that whatever the waters had stirred up, it wouldn't be a good thing.

An hour later Kyra stood in a secluded spot halfway between the state lab in Pikesville and the Pennsylvania border looking at a swampy patch of ground. "Some bird-watchers reported this, if you can believe that," the detective sergeant told her, shaking his head. His salt-and-pepper hair marked him as someone who'd been in the job awhile, he'd probably seen this sort of thing before. "I'm hoping that we can have a day or two before the media gets hold of the news, at least. That, or maybe I'm wrong and what I'm seeing aren't human bones."

"I don't think you're wrong," Kyra said, her heart sinking. "What we're looking at is most likely human remains."

"I guess we could always hope that we're real lucky and maybe this is just an Indian burial site, or some forgotten Civil War grave."

Kyra sighed, squatting to examine the scene without touching anything with her gloved hands. "I'm afraid not. This appears to be something much more recent." What she didn't tell the detective was what she'd seen that made her the most distressed. Unless she was seeing things the wrong way, the size of the bones led her to think that whoever had been left here had not been an adult. And to make matters even worse, there appeared to be more than one set of bones. Kyra found herself praying silently as she began to direct her team in their work. It might be days before this was all sorted out, and she would need all the help she could get.

Kyra's heart sank as she gingerly got closer to the ground to examine what was in front of her without contaminating the scene. She'd only been on the job as the state crime lab's chief forensic anthropologist for a few months, and before this her work had been relatively low-key. She rested her gloved fingers on the ground, contemplating the fact that this discovery would change all that in a hurry.

Sighing, she straightened up slowly, careful not to brush against anything. The white coveralls she wore over her street clothes would keep her from leaving too much trace evidence, but she always liked to err on the side of caution. Kyra hadn't gotten to her position in the state crime lab by being careless.

"Let me get my photo crew in here. When they're done, we'll start taking things out slowly."

"How slowly?" The detective looked up, scanning the sky. "It's not that late in the day. I was hoping we might get this finished before dark."

Kyra sighed again. "You mean dark today?" She watched the man as his eyebrows rose in consternation.

"It's going to take you that long?"

"At least two days, probably. That's if everything goes smoothly, which never happens. And it's going to be slow, painstaking work."

"Great. Now tell me how we keep this from being a media feeding frenzy by the end of tomorrow."

Kyra shrugged. "My job is just to do this right. I can't help you with the media. You'll have to deal with them all by yourself."

"Tell me why I shouldn't arrest you." The uniformed officer glared at Joshua Richards, who tried to focus through the haze before his eyes. "Your license doesn't match the name you've already given me and your story makes no sense."

"Call the number I gave you. The person who answers will back me up." Josh's head throbbed and his right shoulder was going to ache for days. When had he gotten to the point where just doing his job hurt this much? Thirty-five was too young to think of himself as middle-aged, wasn't it? Tonight he wasn't so sure.

The officer's answering laugh was short, dismissive. "Convenient. Probably a buddy on a cell phone. I bet you've got a deal…when he gets in trouble you'd do the same for him, right?"

"It's not like that. Call the number. It's my unit chief in the bureau."

"Sure. And he'll say…"

"She. Special Agent Gorman is a she."

"Even better. She'll say that Joshua Richards…if that's your real name…"

"It's my real name," Josh said through clenched teeth, trying not to let his temper get the better of him again. He still couldn't believe that he'd been so out of it that when the officer first asked for his name, he'd blurted out a last name that he hadn't used since he was eleven. What kind of Freudian slip was that?

"Sure. Whatever. Anyway, she'll say you're a great guy and you were just doing your civic duty here, cleaning up the streets even though you just happened to be loaded to the gills."

Joshua fought the urge to wince; it would only make his head and shoulder hurt worse. And if he caused himself more pain he'd lose even more control. That would probably convince this officer that he really was as impaired by alcohol as the man seemed to think Josh was. Explaining the truth would be far more difficult. The man in uniform looked as if he was just experienced enough not to accept the truth; that most of the reek of liquor on Josh was splashed on his clothes, not from drinking the stuff.

Still, in his undercover role on this investigation he couldn't have totally avoided a drink at the bar. He would have been more conspicuous without one than with something in front of him. So he'd had a little bit to drink, as little as possible. Still, he didn't normally drink by choice, and the alcohol coupled with a shortage of sleep and the nagging disappointment he felt with life made for a dangerous combination.

So instead of staying low profile undercover he'd gotten himself into a fight. Not only had he lost, but his stupidity could cost the bureau five months of hard work, and put his job in jeopardy. As he mulled this over, the officer in charge was making a call on his phone. From what Josh could hear the man had finally taken him seriously and called Ms. Gorman. The discussion was short and to the point. When the officer finished, his expression looked thoughtful.

"Okay, so maybe you were telling the truth. At least that was convincing enough that I won't arrest you. But if that was really your boss I don't envy you the day you're going to have tomorrow." The man's grim smile made Josh's head throb even harder.

He drove home carefully, using little-traveled roads and side streets even after he'd bought coffee and something to eat to counteract the alcohol in his system. Pam Gorman was going to skin him alive in the office tomorrow, and he probably deserved every bit of what she gave him. His life was spiraling downward as he watched.

What did he do now? For a brief, flashing moment the cool, dark sanctuary of a church in Illinois flashed through his mind. The place had been far from welcoming; at least it seemed cold and remote in the memories he'd carried around for nearly a quarter century. Kneeling there in a back pew was the last time Josh remembered praying.

"What do You want me to do?" he asked out loud into the darkness. He got no clear sense of an answer. Still, what he'd said was like a prayer. Maybe it even *was* a prayer. All Josh knew for sure is that he needed to talk to somebody. Here in the dark in his car talking to God sounded about as reasonable as anything else.

"I need help. For the first time in my life I feel like I can't make it on my own and I don't know where to go." Josh ran out of words at that point, and it was starting to feel strange to talk out loud in the car to someone he wasn't sure existed. Still, it gave him an odd sense of peace and he went home wondering what would happen next.

Four days after the phone call that took her out to the park, Kyra was back in her lab. Piecing together what the team had found in the flood-damaged park might take weeks. The bones were still being gently cleaned and treated, every possible hint of evidence being gleaned from them and from the scene before she would start the arduous task of trying to figure out what had happened. It could take another two or three weeks from that point just to be able to give a reasonable estimate of who the people they'd found had been. And even then, identification would be sketchy. Nothing that could have identified any particular individual easily had turned up at the site. No purses, wallets or other identification came out of the mud; only a few scraps of mostly rotted clothing. Time and the elements had been on the side of whoever had concealed these deaths.

I could really use some help here, Lord, Kyra prayed silently as she looked at the puzzle in front of her. Already she felt a responsibility to find the answers to who these people had been in life, where they belonged. Part of that was simple: they were children of God who hadn't deserved to be left dead or nearly dead out in a deserted field someplace. But now she would have to find out if they had enough evidence to discover if the three partial skulls they'd found belonged to the only victims. *Please,* she prayed, *show me the way to give glory to You and dignity to these children.* It was going to take an incredible amount of effort and more work than she was capable of doing alone.

As Kyra bent over the stainless-steel lab table to examine the first few pieces of bone released to her, she was aware of someone standing behind her. "Allie?" she asked softly, not wanting to take her eyes off the task at hand.

"Yes, Doctor…I mean, Kyra. I hate to bring you another problem, but you got an e-mail from one of the lieutenants that I think I need to read to you." Kyra got so much e-mail each day that her assistant did some of the sorting and prioritizing. If she said this one had to be heard right now, it must be fairly urgent.

Allie's voice sounded small and hesitant, at odds with the young woman's normally confident demeanor and businesslike gray slacks and pale blue oxford blouse under her white lab coat. Communication from somebody at that rank in the state police did not normally mean good news.

"Just give me the worst of it if you want to," Kyra said, laying out delicate hand bones and trying to determine whether they all might have come from the same person.

"Okay. Well." There was a pause as if Allie was scanning the message she held. "What it boils down to is that the state and the federal parks people are arguing over who should be handling this case. The land where everything was found is right on the border of the park where it meets some state property."

Kyra groaned. "Don't tell me they're going to take this away from us now." The hardest work of recovering the evidence had already been done, and amazingly the media hadn't caught wind of things yet. Even though she felt a little overwhelmed by the task at hand, she didn't want to let go of the challenge just yet. Without media attention she could probably get a good week of work in and be much closer to identifying these kids.

There was a little more silence from Allie while papers rustled. "Not exactly. It kind of looks like they want to let you handle the investigation and run it out of the state lab, but give you some help."

"Oh, great. I've had federal government 'help' before and it can get mighty tricky. In fact, I can only think of one really helpful federal employee I've ever met…" Kyra's words trailed off as she felt her cheeks flush pink. Thinking about that particular person stirred her up more than working with these bones. She definitely didn't want to turn around and face Allie right this minute, or even prolong this particular train of thought long enough for her perceptive assistant to ask who she was talking about.

"Well, I hope his name is Joshua Richards, then," Allie said, causing Kyra to raise her head quickly, banging into the bright light she'd lowered to give herself some aid in seeing distinctions in the bone. "Because that's who they're sending to help you."

What was that old phrase? Kyra asked herself as she rubbed the back of her head where it had struck the stainless-steel lamp. Oh, right. *Be careful what you pray for, because you just might get it.* "No one can tell me God doesn't have a sense of humor," Kyra muttered under her breath. Maybe next time she would frame her request for help a little more specifically.

She realized that Allie was still standing behind her, waiting for some kind of answer. She tried to calm herself down. "That's okay, I guess. I know him, anyway, and he's a good investigator. Or at least he used to be." There'd been some talk of a personal crisis a while back, before she'd left the university, but Kyra couldn't remember exactly what had happened. They'd grown close during an investigation a year ago, and then drawn apart just as quickly. "So how quickly should I expect this help, anyway?"

"Soon. It looks like the lieutenant sent you an e-mail instead of a letter because they expect Agent Richards by the end of the week."

"But it's already Wednesday," Kyra said, trying not to let her voice rise any higher toward panic pitch. She needed more than a day or two to prepare mentally to work with Joshua Richards again. He was attractive and disturbing and she didn't need to deal with either of those things right now.

"Very astute, Dr. Elliott," a deep voice drawled from the doorway. Kyra bumped her head on the light overhead for the second time in less than ten minutes, which was definitely going to leave her with a sore spot. So much for that day or two to prepare, Kyra thought. Joshua was here now whether she liked it or not.

TWO

Josh looked around the sterile space that passed for Kyra Elliott's office. "So, you took this job voluntarily?" he asked, trying not to sound skeptical. The whole building was new, but had no charm or personality. Everything was concrete and steel, probably easy to keep clean and contamination-free, but even starker than he remembered Kyra's university lab being.

"I most certainly did," she answered, chin stuck out as if asking for an argument. "They were looking for someone to expand their forensic anthropology department and I was drawn to the prospect of doing criminal work full time."

He turned that over in his mind, trying to make sense of it. Kyra hardly looked old enough to have her doctorate in forensic science, much less be a sought-after expert in her field. Sure, he'd used her skills when he'd needed some off-beat knowledge for the FBI more than once. And he probably owed her a great deal for helping put his personal quest to an end. Still, she looked more like an undergrad in biology with her willowy frame and huge green eyes. He even remembered one case they'd worked on together in Indiana where they'd almost been denied entrance to a restaurant with a bar attached because the manager had to be convinced that Kyra was really over twenty-one.

"I guess I could ask you the same thing," Kyra said, drawing his attention back to the present. "Did you actually volunteer for this particular assignment?" Her brow furrowed as she leaned back in her high-backed desk chair, and then she smiled slightly. "You didn't, did you? Joshua, what did you do or say to somebody in the bureau to get you shunted over here?"

Joshua felt his cheeks flush. "You don't want to know," he told her, meaning every word of it. He had no desire to tell Kyra all the stupid choices he'd made in the last eight months. He was probably lucky that the worst his actions had earned him was this dead-end investigator's assignment. If this was the answer to that prayer or whatever it had been in his car a few days ago, it was a pretty goofy answer. "So fill me in on what we've got so far. Nobody at the bureau seemed to have a lot of information."

"That's because there isn't much yet. Some birdwatchers in a park were tracking something rare when they came upon bones stirred up by the spring floods. We've recovered about all we're going to. We're cleaning the bones carefully, and I'm trying to sort out how many individuals are involved. If I had to speculate at this point, I'd say we're looking at three young women somewhere between twelve and eighteen."

Josh tried to stifle the groan he felt building, but wasn't entirely successful. "But that's just speculation, right? And you don't even know for sure how long these victims have been dead."

"There were just enough remnants of clothing that I can tell you they'd probably been there no longer than twelve years, and probably not less than seven. So I can head off any questions about this being an ancient burial site, or Civil War remains. Believe me, you're not the first person to hope for that. These were kids who were alive in the early nineties for sure."

"How long before you can get more specific than all this?" He stopped himself before saying more, like "all this guessing" because he knew that would only stir up the scientist in Kyra.

"We'll have a few more answers by Monday. At least by then I will know for sure how many people we're talking about, and probably give you a better estimate of age, size and ethnic makeup."

"So what do you want me to do until then?" Josh dreaded her answer, because it was likely to involve a lot of pointless, boring research.

Kyra huffed. "I know that look, Agent Richards. You're already bored with this assignment and it hasn't even started yet. I suggest you get used to the idea that you need to spend the next few days searching for statistics on teens that have gone missing in the time period we're targeting. If you want to make it easier on yourself, just start with the Baltimore-Washington corridor in the most likely four years."

How did she do that? Josh had forgotten how quickly Kyra tuned into his ways of thinking, and how different they were in their opinions. He sat up straighter in the office chair and tried to look more attentive. "Is there a spare office for me to use?"

Kyra shrugged. "Afraid not. We've got researchers doubling up already in this department. I can let you have a corner in here." Her quick smile gave Joshua a start of surprise. "That way I can keep an eye on you and make sure you're really checking out the missing kids' stats."

"Great," he said weakly. Maybe this assignment would teach him to improve his attitude with his supervisors in the bureau. A few weeks of working closely with Kyra Elliott would either reform him or send him over the edge.

Kyra studied Josh Richards as he sat working at the laptop she'd been able to provide for him his second day on the job. He'd been in her office two days now and she was still taking in the difference in him since the last time they'd been on a case together over a year ago. Before, Josh had been sharp and distant with most people, focused on the particulars of his job and little else. But he'd had self-confidence that oozed out his pores to go along with that aloof attitude. Kyra had always wanted to try to get past the aloofness and explore the person with the attitude, but he never let that happen.

Now Joshua sat in his office chair, close to the

computer. He was so quiet; no music playing, nothing personal to brighten this corner he worked in. There was almost a defeated slump to his shoulders, a posture that Kyra would never have associated with Josh before. "How's it going?" she asked softly from where she sat a few feet away doing paperwork.

"Okay, I guess," he said without looking up. "There are a couple of dozen missing teens listed in the corridor during those four years you pointed out. If you're sure your victims are female, that takes out a few but leaves plenty more. Any ideas yet how many we're looking at?"

"I think we have three individuals," Kyra said, trying to give Josh a reminder that these were people they were talking about. "And they're definitely female. I can tell from the brow ridges on the skulls and the size and shape of the pelvic bones."

Joshua winced but didn't turn away from his computer. "I guess that narrows it down a little bit. How specific are you going to be able to get, anyway?"

"You'll probably be surprised by how much I'll probably be able to tell you," Kyra told him. "Haven't you ever hung out with any of the forensic experts at the bureau?"

Joshua shook his head, and Kyra noticed that the light caught small glints of silver in the ginger of his temples. That was new and it disturbed her a little. What kind of stress did that to someone who had to be in his mid-thirties? "Not by choice. For the most part I took the information they had to give me and went back to my own investigations."

Ouch. They were definitely going to have to work on Josh's attitude toward people. Kyra tried to think of ways to help him start seeing the individual nature of those around him, whether they were crime victims or fellow workers. Maybe a little education was the answer. "Do you want to know more?" Kyra wasn't sure what his response was going to be, or why she was so interested. In the past two days Joshua had come in on time, done his job quietly and left when the rest of the day shift did. If he'd gotten to know anyone yet it would be news to her.

"I'm not sure. What would that entail?" His normally pale face appeared even paler. Why hadn't she ever noticed that he had a dusting of light freckles across his cheekbones? As his face blanched a little, they stood out in relief.

"Depends on how much you want to know. I won't force you into anything you don't want to be part of." Kyra gave him a quick smile, expecting him to answer with one in return, but he stayed solemn. "I think most of it is really interesting, but not everybody does." She thought about bringing up the young state policeman a few days back, but held back. That might just bring out Josh's competitive nature and she didn't want him doing anything just to prove that he could best somebody else.

"I'd like to know a little more, but I'll warn you up front that I don't handle detailed medical stuff very well. I know there won't be blood involved here, but there have to be plenty of other things that will bother me in your labs."

"That's possible. I'll sketch things out in broad terms for you and if you want to know more about an area, ask me, okay?"

Josh nodded, a tiny bit of color coming back into his face. His shoulders began to lower from the tense position they'd held almost up to his ears, and he looked like somebody who was really listening.

She took a deep breath and prayed silently for guidance and wisdom. "So, the first thing that we do when all we've got to work with is bones is try to find as many teeth as possible. Even if we can't match dental records to a victim, the condition of their mouth tells us a lot about who they were."

Josh's brow wrinkled for a minute, and then his expression cleared. "Okay, that makes sense. I guess people out on the fringes of things don't really have great dental insurance or anything, do they?"

"They don't." Kyra was glad that he had picked up on what she said this quickly. "When you're down on your luck there are a lot of things more important than dental care, like eating and having a roof over your head. We can also tell a lot about age from looking at somebody's teeth. If their third molars have erupted they're probably past eighteen."

"Third molars. Does that mean wisdom teeth?" He really did catch on fast. Now, if she could just somehow steer that intellect into learning a little compassion...

"Right. And one of the reasons I could figure out that these three girls were younger than eighteen was that none of them show any signs of having wisdom teeth coming through to the surface."

"What if you don't have any teeth?"

"Then it's a lot harder to come up with an individual's identity. We can figure out whether they're male or female, and approximate size and age, but without teeth most skeletons are hard to identify. The only other help is if someone has had some kind of bone reconstruction that led to plates or rods being left in their body, or if injuries that show up on X rays leave a mark."

"Do you have enough teeth to identify these three girls?" Kyra still wasn't sure if his question came out of concern or merely the hope that the work he was doing wouldn't be in vain.

"I think so. At least two of the three have had some dental work, so if we can match up X rays of a missing person we'll be okay."

"And the third one?"

"That's going to be a bit more difficult. She should have gotten some dental work, but never did. There are unfilled cavities in a couple of her teeth and she could have used braces. I'm working on one angle that may help identify her, though."

"Okay, you just admitted that without teeth or dental records it's hard to identify somebody. Did she have broken bones, or some kind of screws somewhere?"

"No, but hers is probably the most recent of the three sets of bones to be left where they were. And there's one other identification help if you're dealing with female bones." She stopped there, giving Josh a little time to figure out what she was talking about on his own.

He had his thoughtful look, then sadness flashed across his features. "You just said all of these girls were probably under eighteen, right? The only other thing I can think of that bones could tell you would be if they'd given birth. That's awfully young, isn't it?"

Kyra felt her emotions spiral back to a place she didn't really want to revisit. It took her a minute or two to gather herself together to answer him. "Younger than most people, but it might help explain the lack of dental work. If this girl was already a mom before her eighteenth birthday, she had lots of other things on her mind."

Joshua's expression stayed clouded. "And it also means that someplace out there is a kid whose mother never came home one day. For his sake, or hers, I kind of hope she'd given the baby up for adoption."

His statement showed more intensity, and more caring, than Kyra had seen from Josh so far. Maybe helping him care about others wouldn't be as difficult as she'd thought. What he said also made Kyra wonder what his own childhood had been like. It wasn't something she was going to ask him about, at least not yet. When she looked at him again he seemed to be studying her. "What?" she said reflexively, hoping she didn't sound too sharp.

"I don't know. You had a different look on your face there for a minute. Sad and kind of faraway. It's not what I usually see." And with that statement Kyra felt the slow heat of anger and confusion rise in her. How could she be so easy to read?

She gave herself a mental shake and straightened her shoulders. "Well, I guess it's just these kids. I don't let the job get to me too often, because then I'm no use to the very people who need my help the most. But you're right, sixteen or seventeen is too early to have a baby for most young women. I'm not so sure I agree with you on the whole adoption thing. It depends on what kind of family a mom has, how close they are. If an aunt or a grandmother can raise the child, everything is fine."

"That sounds good, but I don't think you really believe it," Josh said, his words back to the flatter tone he'd used most of the time. "Everything isn't going to be fine in a situation that allows the body of a young girl to be missing for seven or eight years without a lot of public outcry." His eyes narrowed as Kyra watched him think.

"You said before that you might know by Monday what ethnic makeup these kids were. How do you figure that out from bones?"

"The differences can be subtle," Kyra admitted. "Different bone densities in some structures, the shape of an eye socket…"

"You can say *orbit*. I know that much. My mom was a nurse." Something about that memory was painful for him, because now Josh was the one to have a brief look of sadness across his face. Kyra filed that away as something else to discuss later.

"Okay. I'm never sure with people whether or not I should keep things simple in case I'm talking way over their heads, or just talk to them the way I would to a colleague. It sounds like you're closer to the colleague level."

"I don't know if I'd go that far, but coming from you that's a compliment. So, colleague, how long are you going to stay and work on all of this tonight?"

Kyra shrugged. "As long as it takes. There's nobody waiting at home except Ranger, and he's pretty self-sufficient."

Joshua's forehead wrinkled. "I don't remember you mentioning a live-in...friend before."

Kyra stifled a giggle. "That's because Ranger's a cat. About fourteen pounds of black fur and attitude who keeps my place free of field mice and crickets, and still doesn't understand after eight years why I won't let him go outside and stalk them out there."

"Oh." Josh smiled faintly. "Well, if you're not going to hurry home to him, would you like to grab dinner someplace? I've heard some of the other staff members talking about a Thai restaurant not too far from here."

"I am hungry. And as long as this is just colleague-to-colleague," Kyra said, giving Josh a pointed look.

"Definitely. I won't even offer to buy your dinner."

"Good. You get back to your computer and I'll shut things down in the next room. I should be ready to go in fifteen minutes."

Remember, just colleague-to-colleague, Kyra reminded herself as she put things to rights in the lab. It might take a lot of work, but she was determined that Josh Richards was never going to know that she thought of him in any other way.

THREE

The Thai restaurant was small, casual and smelled fantastic from the moment Josh walked in. The aroma of chilies, spices and lemongrass filled the air, and he discovered that he was hungry. How long had it been since he had felt truly hungry and interested in food? Then again, how long had it been since he'd had dinner with an attractive young woman, even if she was practically his boss?

He tried not to take it personally when Kyra insisted that they both drive to the restaurant. It wasn't a matter of trust, she explained. "You're going home afterward and I may come back here to work on one last thing."

"I have a feeling there's 'one last thing' a lot of the time," Josh told her, watching her flush with color in an admission that didn't need words to go with it. Kyra's tenacity was what had made them a good team when he'd needed her help in cases for the bureau. So it didn't surprise him that she gave that kind of focus to her work all the time.

"There is," she admitted. "But that doesn't mean I

expect everybody in the lab to work like I do. As long as they give things their best effort, I'm fine with a reasonable work week."

She double-checked to make sure he knew where the restaurant was, and headed toward her car. Josh wasn't sure what he expected to see her get into, but the vintage Ford pickup truck gave him a surprise. When she showed up at the restaurant he intended to ask her about that.

He settled in to wait for her, taking the corner table a young man pointed out, and ordering an iced coffee while he waited. He watched the door of the restaurant, listening to the overhead bell jingle as people came in. Just about the time his drink came, Kyra walked through the door and he was struck by her appearance.

Why hadn't he ever noticed that the woman was downright beautiful? She'd unfastened the clip that held her glossy auburn hair. She must have ridden over from the lab with the window rolled down in the truck. Her cheeks were pink and she looked slightly windblown, refreshed and healthy. Josh mentally contrasted what he must look like; pale skin that hardly ever saw the light of day, lines beginning to etch the corners of his eyes and his workday uniform of a white shirt, dark pants and an extremely sedate tie.

Kyra slid into the seat across from him, looking at his iced coffee. "I should have told you to order me one if you made it here first. I know I probably don't need any more caffeine this late in the day, but I really like those things."

"I'll make a note of it for next time," Josh said, wondering where the words came from as soon as they were out of his mouth. What made him think there was going to be a "next time" with Kyra? She'd made it clear this wasn't a social engagement, just dinner with a workmate. Even an hour ago that wouldn't have bothered him; why did it feel like it mattered now?

In any case, Kyra seemed to ignore his comment. "Cool. Do you like chicken satay? We could split an order while we waited for the rest of dinner."

"Sure." Josh let her order the appetizer and her iced coffee while he thought about ways to ask a few questions about her without seeming overly interested. But his new awareness of Kyra's beauty and the constant reminder that she was basically his boss right now left him tongue-tied for a while.

They ordered their dinners and Kyra made a little small talk while Josh tried not to ask too many questions, even though at least a dozen were running through his mind. The satay came and they probably ate half of it before Kyra looked over at him and smiled.

"Hey, you're mighty quiet," she said. "Once you got me alone outside the labs I expected all kinds of questions."

Josh told himself the flush he felt must be due to the amount of fiery Thai chilies in the peanut dipping sauce. "I don't want to irritate you. You're dealing with enough questions right now just focusing on this case. Do you work like this all the time?"

Kyra shrugged slightly. "When I need to. And I

won't work all weekend. I don't work on Sundays unless it's an emergency and I have no other choice."

"I guess everybody needs some rest. But wouldn't it make more sense just to work through and try to catch a break in the case?"

"Not for me. There are all kinds of reasons that I can get more accomplished in six days than I can in seven. My Sundays are precious to me."

Josh felt his heart sink. "I'll bet you spend them in church, don't you?"

"Not always. But I do try to spend them in ways that bring honor to God, and there aren't too many times that that means hanging out at the lab."

"So where do you go if it's not church?" Josh caught himself leaning forward to hear her answer.

Kyra stirred the straw around in her iced coffee. "All kinds of places. I go horseback riding sometimes, grab ice cream with some friends, maybe even just sit quietly alone or go to the movies with four or five teenage girls."

How was any of this a way to honor God? Josh felt really confused about that. Kyra didn't look confused at all. She appeared perfectly happy with her choices. This discussion was going to take a lot longer to finish than Josh had figured on.

Before he could ask more questions their entrées arrived along with a bowl of rice. "This all looks great," Kyra said with enthusiasm, and she surprised Josh by reaching over and taking the serving spoon in his pad thai.

Maybe she was confused about what she'd ordered. "Hey, Kyra? I think the pad thai is mine," Josh said.

She smiled but didn't put down the spoon. "Well, yeah, but you're okay with sharing, right? I think sharing dinner is fun. It gives us both something new to try."

This was totally outside his experience. "I guess. It's just a little different for me."

Kyra giggled softly. "What's the matter? Don't bureau people share their food? Or don't you like green curry? I didn't get it too hot, honest."

When he didn't answer right away, Kyra looked more serious. "This really isn't something you're used to doing, is it? If it makes you uncomfortable, I'll just stick to my own dish and you can have yours. Sorry."

She started to put down the spoon, and Josh found himself reaching over gently and taking her wrist. "No, it's okay. You're right, it's not something I usually do. I just didn't grow up in a sharing kind of environment. And you are correct about the other part, too, because bureau folks are pretty protective about their property, including food."

"That's too bad," Kyra said with a soft smile. "They're missing out on a lot."

"I imagine so." Josh looked down to realize he was still holding on to her wrist and let it go. "But I think it's time I stopped missing out." He took the spoon in the rice and served himself a little, spooning the fragrant green curry on top of it. Kyra's answering grin lifted his spirits like nothing had in days.

Later, after coconut ice cream, Kyra argued when

he told her he was going to follow her back to the lab. She stood in the parking lot near her truck with her arms crossed, frowning slightly. Josh explained, "I know you're no delicate flower who needs constant protection, but I was raised to treat women a certain way. If that bothers you, I apologize in advance, but it won't keep me from following you back to the lab if you're going to go back to work."

"I'm definitely going back," Kyra told him. "Although, after this dinner I'm not sure how long I'll be able to work before I'll want to go home and doze. Ranger will like that."

Josh struggled to find something to say to that. With his allergy to pets he wasn't real enthused about Kyra having a cat. At least she hadn't brought enough cat dander into the office to make his eyes water. "Once you're in the building, I'll head home," he told her. "I just want to make sure everything is all right."

Her answering hug was brief but warm and the surprise of her giving it to him rocked him back slightly on his heels. "You're sweet and I won't argue. Thanks." In a moment she was in her truck and Josh walked quickly to his car so that he could follow her as he'd promised. Around him the jasmine notes of her cologne filled his senses and followed him the rest of the evening through his drive to the lab and all the way home.

Everything was gone. It was Saturday morning and the Watcher stood in the mud under the trees at the park, looking in surprise at the yellow caution tape surrounding several shallow impressions in the earth. What had happened here? The last time he'd visited, the two bird-watchers were calling the police, but he hadn't expected this much action this quickly. All they could have found were a few unconnected bones.

Now that the tall weeds and scrawny saplings that had grown up in his private garden had been washed away by the spring rains, it looked like a different place. Having the police mess around with things on top of that made it unrecognizable. His things were gone. Or at least they'd been uncovered from their hiding places. Somebody had found them, that was certain. The yellow tape and spindly orange plastic fencing might have been made to look like this was just an area the parks service was trying to keep people out of because the ground was swampy, but he knew differently.

How dare they mess everything up! This was his place, with his secrets. Now what was he supposed to do? As he stood there wondering, there was a rustle behind him, and a voice called tentatively. "Sir? I'm going to have to ask you not to go any closer to the fenced area. If you're bird-watching, we're directing people over to the South Trail."

For a moment the Watcher felt as if he was going to jump out of his skin. "What? Oh, sure." Relief washed over him as he realized that to the young park ranger, or whatever he was, the binoculars around his neck and his nondescript jeans and shirt made him look like any other guy out to enjoy a Saturday in the park. "Sorry, Officer. I wasn't trying to do anything illegal."

The kid smiled. "Don't worry, you haven't done anything wrong yet. I'm just supposed to keep people from getting into areas like that one where it's too swampy for us to be sure of your safety. And I'm not an officer or anything, just working here for the summer." The kid pointed toward his yellow name badge and the Watcher could see that it gave the kid's name below the bright green line that proclaimed him a volunteer. So he hadn't done anything yet, huh? Wouldn't this kid be surprised if he knew? But with any luck, he wasn't going to know, and neither was anybody else. The Watcher tried to walk nonchalantly away from this ruined place. Somebody was going to pay for this; he just needed to find out who was responsible.

It was time to go home and look through the newspapers to see what the police said about their finds. That would tell him who had dug up his treasures. Didn't they realize that it would be their fault when he started hunting again? Without his secrets here, how could anybody expect him to access his memories? Now it would be time to find a new place, and new things to fill that place, even sooner than he'd planned.

By ten o'clock on Saturday morning, Kyra's back ached. Her shoulders tightened with the focus of her efforts with the magnifier and the smaller pieces of bone. Sometimes when she was busy like this she remembered Gran sifting through a jigsaw puzzle. The difference was that Gran did her puzzles for fun, humming softly while she matched the pieces. Kyra did her work in a much more serious way, but the painstaking business of matching the pieces was the same. And when she finished putting together one of her "puzzles" it could mean closure for a family somewhere who finally knew where their loved one was.

More bone pieces, and larger ones, were coming out of the cleaning room now. In the work area she'd set aside just for this purpose, Kyra kept turning bones in different directions, angling them slightly while examining their color and texture. They'd separated out the pieces that were most likely human at the dump site. Bringing them back to the lab allowed Kyra and her researchers to separate out anything that wasn't human bone.

Now, after the cleaning, it became clearer which pieces went together. The set of bones that went back the farthest had softer details around the edges and an entirely different color to their surface from the ones that had been in the ground a shorter time.

Each set of skeletal pieces that Kyra wanted to keep separate had its own gurney, arranged in a horseshoe so that she could have easy access between the three steel gurneys. If anyone asked, the skeletons were just A, B and C, but already to Kyra they were Abigail, Bethany and Chloe. She prayed that some day soon she could give these girls back their real names, but until then she wanted to do all that she could to make them living human beings in her own mind.

As she identified what seemed to be two of Chloe's metacarpals, the door to the room swung slightly on silent hinges, making Kyra jump a little. "Who's there?"

Her voice sounded a little high and sharp in her own ears. She wasn't used to having much company on Saturdays.

Josh came through the doorway with a grimace. "Sorry. I didn't even think about startling you. I knew you'd be here, and frankly, I ran out of things to do at home so I decided to come in and try to get something done."

Kyra looked at Josh, realizing that this was the first time that she'd seen him out of his weekday uniform of dark pants and a white shirt. Today he wore khakis and a sportier shirt, and no tie, either. "That's okay. I was so focused on this set of bones and what they're telling me that I didn't expect anybody to come in."

His brow wrinkled a little. "I have to admit that it's really strange to me to hear you talking about bones telling you anything. Frankly, I don't even know how you can tell which ones belong to which...set."

His pause told Kyra that Josh still didn't think about Chloe and the others as real people yet. It would probably take an identification of at least one set of the bones for Josh to see any of them as a girl who had lived, grown, had sorrows and joys like anybody else, and then died. She sighed softly. "They tell me quite a bit, Josh. And explaining how I can tell one person's remains from another might take me a couple of hours. Once I've worked through everything we've collected, maybe I can show you."

He nodded slightly. "Sure. I understand that you can't do it right now. Getting as much done as you can makes more sense. Meanwhile, I'll go in and sort through some more missing persons reports on the computer." He crossed the room, heading for the door that led to Kyra's office. "Does anybody make coffee on weekends?"

"Sometimes. There aren't many of us in today, though, and nobody's gotten around to it. I'd welcome a cup if you get some going," she told him.

"That I can do," Josh said, with a ghost of a smile on his lips. "In my department at the bureau, making decent coffee was a survival skill not dependent on gender or rank within the department. If we could have talked them into a cappuccino maker I could have run that, too."

He looked around into the corners of the room. "I know this is a brand-new set of labs. I don't suppose…"

Kyra had to grin. "Nope, the State of Maryland barely sprang for regular coffeemakers. Weekdays when everything is open, I think there's a cart in the lobby closest to the cafeteria that serves foo-foo coffee."

That brought a laugh out of Joshua for the first time. "Foo-foo coffee, huh? After that iced coffee last night I figured you for a vanilla latte kind of person. Guess I was wrong."

"Guess you were," she said, trying to focus on her work. "When I'm not eating Thai or Vietnamese food, straight, black coffee in any insulated container that keeps it hot and prevents me from spilling it is my beverage of choice."

He gave her a mock salute. "Ready in ten minutes,

ma'am. I'll even wash the mug." Before she could reply he was through the doorway and out of sight, leaving Kyra to wonder what part of what she'd said had tickled Josh. He had a nice laugh. Too bad he didn't use it more often.

She'd puzzled out two bits of Bethany's foot, and what she thought was her left orbital arch, when Josh slid back into the room as quietly as the first time, making her startle again. "Any chance we can get you to wear a bell or something?" she groused. "You're just too quiet."

"It's a talent I need when I'm doing undercover work. Besides, people reveal a lot more about themselves when they don't think anybody's there. For example, you tend to stick just the tip of your tongue out at the corner of your mouth when you're trying to figure something out."

Kyra had a flash of irritation as he handed her the warm travel mug. She was tempted to make some smart remark, but the truth was that Josh was right. "Thanks for the coffee," she said, trying not to sound too irritated. Being astute was part of his job. She realized that she could probably use his gifts of perception about people to explain to him how she knew things just from looking at the bones in front of her. But first, she wanted to sip some of this coffee and stretch to get the kinks out of her neck. Deep concentration on these small bones left her physically pained after a while.

When she looked back at him, Josh had a thoughtful look on his face. "What?" she asked, hoping he'd tell her what he was thinking.

"You look uncomfortable. How many more hours can you lean over that kind of close work without making yourself sore for days?"

Kyra shrugged, still trying to get some of the kinks out. "A few. I think I'm close to a breakthrough here, so I'll keep at it. If I can find a few more facial bones on…gurney B," she said, unwilling to tell Josh about the names she'd given the girls, "we might have enough to start looking for medical records."

"Don't you always need teeth for that?"

"It helps," Kyra admitted. "But I think I'm seeing a pattern of some old, healed facial injuries in this one skeleton. It's the kind of thing that would have given her a distinctive look, and probably left a legal trail as well."

Josh's expression clouded. "You said these bones probably belonged to teenagers. If the injuries you've found are healed, you're thinking child abuse, aren't you?"

"It's one of the top reasons for fractures in kids, unfortunately. I wish I could say it wasn't."

"Yeah, me too." He turned around, then appeared to reconsider leaving and faced her again. For a moment he stood silently. "How can you see stuff like this and still believe in God? What kind of God lets little kids get beaten up?"

"God didn't beat up this child. A human being is responsible for that," Kyra said with more fervor than necessary. "If you want to see what God can do in a kid's life, then come with me tomorrow."

"To church?" Josh asked, a challenge in his steely eyes.

"No, to the mall for a movie. Bring money for popcorn and ice cream after the show."

"Sure." His quick acceptance surprised Kyra. She'd expected him to put up an argument.

"And clean out the backseat of your car if you need to," she instructed. "My truck will only hold two besides me. You've got seat belts for three in the backseat, don't you?"

"Yes." He raised one eyebrow, seeming to ask what he was getting himself into. "What were you going to do before I came along?"

"I have no idea," Kyra admitted. "I figured that if God wanted me to take all of the kids to the movies, then a way to take them all would show up."

"And you got me instead," Josh said. Kyra didn't have the heart to tell him that she thought he was exactly what God had in mind. Josh was nowhere near ready to hear something like that.

FOUR

What on earth had he been thinking? Josh asked himself for at least the tenth time in an hour. Why had he agreed to meet Kyra and take strange teenagers to the mall? He didn't know the first thing about teens, and especially not girls. The three in his backseat were giggling and making strange noises and speaking some language beyond his understanding, full of phrases like "and then he went yeah and I went no way" while he tried to keep concentrating on Kyra, navigating in the front seat to guide him to a mall he'd never been to.

He'd found the parking lot of Kyra's church, where they'd agreed to meet, with no trouble. He wished that Kyra had let him pick her up at home, but she had argued that this was a more central location and closer to where they needed to get the girls. So he'd agreed and shown up on time, hoping that his weekend casual khakis were all right for the afternoon.

Probably to put the girls at ease, Kyra wore jeans and a soft sweater the color of honey, picking up golden notes in her glossy auburn hair. The uniform of the day in the backseat was jeans with baggy sweatshirt jackets that Kyra called hoodies.

Only when they were all getting out of the car in the mall's parking garage did Josh notice that one of his passengers was pregnant. The realization hit him hard; none of these girls looked to be more than fifteen. Kyra chatted with them as if they were old friends, while all three eyed him warily.

"Now, understand that I chose the movie today," Kyra said to him as they walked to the theater. She talked loudly enough so that the whole group could hear her, even though she was speaking to Josh. "Marta, Ashley and Jasmine are all far too mature to want to see an animated movie, but it was my turn to pick, so they're humoring me." The girls nodded vigorously and Josh fought hard to hide any hint of a smile.

He could still remember being thirteen and trying to act tough all the time. If he went to the movies back then, it was always with his sister. At that age it was nice to have Chrissie to blame for them going to watch kid movies. That way he had an excuse in case he saw any of his friends at the movie theater. It had been years later before Josh realized that any friends he met were trying just as hard as he was to maintain a "cool" image. In those days before twelve-screen theaters everybody was there to see one of two or three shows. And back then the ticket sellers were stringent about keeping kids out of R-rated films. Not that Josh would have tried to sneak into one, especially not with Chrissie in tow.

So here he was, surrounded with a gaggle of giggling females who were trying their hardest to act as cool as he had more than over twenty years ago. He suspected they were all secretly glad that Kyra had picked a kids' movie. That way they could see it without any of their friends thinking that they had chosen to go there. Josh figured it made them happy to have a friend like Kyra who took them to the movies, too. From what Kyra had told him of the kids' backgrounds, everybody was in foster care or the juvenile-justice system; some of them both.

Today, though, they were just teens going to the mall, and Josh could feel their excitement and high spirits even when they weren't talking. He looked at one of the family groups passing by them and wondered what those people saw. More than likely they wondered why a middle-aged man was shepherding a bunch of teenage girls at the mall, because Kyra didn't look much older than the kids in some ways. She had the same lighthearted expression, smiling as she pointed something out in a window to Jasmine that made all the girls comment.

"Hey, Josh. I mean, Mr. Richards," one of the girls said to him, pulling him out of his fog. "Are you going to spring for popcorn for all of us, or just Kyra? Lunch at the house was pretty bad and I can already taste that buttered popcorn. But if you're just going to treat your date…"

"Ashley, what makes you think this is a date? We're just doing a Sunday movie, same as usual. And don't go trying to talk my friend into buying you popcorn." Kyra still used a light tone so the girl didn't feel like she was in trouble.

Marta leaned in close next to Ashley. "Not a date, huh? It's the only time you've ever brought anybody along for a movie that wasn't a church lady. He's definitely no church lady." Marta had an impish grin that made the other girls laugh and Kyra turn a little pink.

"C'mon you two. I want to see a movie and have popcorn. If you keep hassling Kyra she'll take us back and we won't get anything. I don't feel like going back, I feel like having a good time. And maybe even ice cream after the movie." Jasmine put a hand on her stomach. "We never get ice cream."

"That's because you should be concentrating on fruit and veggies, not popcorn and ice cream," Kyra said breezily. "But you're right, if you keep speculating on my personal life, you're more likely to leave without enjoying your afternoon."

Jasmine put a hand on her hip and glared at her friends. "See? I told you. Now, be good so we can see the movie." The other two girls grimaced, but they stopped teasing Kyra. Josh marveled at how fast the situation was defused.

In the lobby of the theater Josh turned to Kyra and spoke softly. "Can they still have popcorn? I like popcorn with my movie, too, and I'm not about to eat in front of those kids unless I'm feeding them."

Kyra smiled. "Just don't make it super-large size, light on the butter, no candy and water instead of soda, got it?"

"Got it." Josh didn't know when the thought of spending thirty dollars on somebody else's snacks made him feel this good. He was beginning to see why Kyra did things like take these kids to a show. It didn't take all that much to make them happy, and watching them smile lifted his spirits as well.

Once they had their snacks, Kyra ushered everybody into the theater, putting the girls in a short row on the left side of the theater, sitting next to them herself and leaving Josh the end seat. "Tricky," he murmured as they settled in. "This way nobody gets out without you knowing about it."

"That's the idea. We can all have a good time without me having to ride herd on the girls all afternoon. They're pretty good kids for the most part, and I want to give them as many chances to succeed as I can."

"I like your attitude," Josh told her. "I wish…more people I know felt that way." He hoped Kyra didn't catch his hesitation; he had almost said he wished that his own mother had felt that way. That was water under the bridge, though. No sense having Kyra feel sorry for him.

After several previews the movie finally started, and Josh found himself actually enjoying it. Animation had improved a great deal since he'd seen a movie like this. A few minutes into the movie he was surprised to feel Kyra's head resting on his shoulder. At first he didn't look over toward her, wondering what she was doing. This was his boss; it was hard to think that she was relaxing by leaning on his shoulder. He had to admit that it felt good, though.

Kyra still leaned against him and there was a weight to her as if she was very relaxed. The scent of her shampoo drifted over him, herbal and warm. When he turned his head a little, Joshua's bubble was burst. Kyra's eyes were closed and she was breathing softly, clearly having dozed off. Jasmine, sitting next to her, looked over at Kyra and smiled briefly at Josh, mouthing "Don't wake her up" to him.

It wasn't often that he took advice from a fifteen-year-old, but this time Josh decided she was right. Kyra had been pushing herself incredibly hard in her quest to identify the skeletons in the lab. With her dozing on his shoulder, Josh felt a strong desire to protect her, take care of her and let her sleep. He slowly eased himself back in the seat to put her in the best position possible, settling in to watch the movie and listen to her soft, regular breathing.

"I can't believe you let me sleep through the movie," Kyra said, still trying to clear her head half an hour after the lights came up in the theater. She felt so embarrassed that she could hardly talk. What was worse—that she'd failed to supervise the girls, or that she'd spent more than an hour sleeping soundly and comfortably while leaning against Josh? He didn't seem to be upset over the incident, and in fact was still grinning slightly as they sat with the girls around a table in the food court eating frozen yogurt.

"You've been working so hard you need the rest,"

he said. "And I woke you up before the lights came back on, didn't I?"

"Yes, but you should have woken me up once you realized I was asleep. You shouldn't have had to be in charge."

"Hey, I did a good job. Nobody got lost, or had too much popcorn or got in trouble. I think it was a good afternoon. And we all enjoyed the movie, too."

Kyra felt prickles of irritation. Why couldn't he agree with her? She hadn't fulfilled her responsibility and she'd fallen asleep on his shoulder. She looked hard at Josh's shirt. Hopefully she hadn't drooled on him while she slept. That was the only thing she could think of that would make the situation more embarrassing.

She looked at Josh and noticed he was smiling. "What?" It almost felt as if he could read her mind.

"You're letting your yogurt melt," he said, still grinning a little. "Should I have gotten you coffee instead?"

Kyra shook her head and looked down at her chocolate frozen yogurt. It was hard to stay upset with somebody who was being that solicitous of her feelings. "No, I'm good. I still think you let me sleep way too long."

He reached over and patted her arm. "Really, don't worry about it. Isn't this supposed to be your day of rest, anyway?"

Kyra wasn't sure whether to be glad that Josh understood that much about her faith, or concerned that he didn't quite get the whole concept. The girls were probably listening to them, so she tried to come up with an answer that would benefit them as well.

"Yes, but it doesn't mean napping when I'm supposed to be doing something else. The Sabbath is supposed to be spent doing things that give glory to God, and rest and renewal to me. I can actually see how taking the kids to a movie and out for frozen yogurt does that, but drooling on your shoulder, not so much."

"Now, you didn't drool. Not at all."

Well, that was a relief, Kyra thought. She knew Josh was honest, and if he said she didn't drool, then it was true. A giggle bordering on a shriek from the adjoining table drew her attention away from Josh. Ashley must have said something that tickled the other two, and they were getting fairly loud. "Let's turn down the volume just a little," Kyra told them. Ashley nodded and Jasmine and Marta busied themselves with their root beer floats.

"We need to get back fairly soon. This is a fifteen-minute warning before we head for home."

Marta made a disgusted noise. "Come on, Kyra. That is *so* not home you're taking us back to. You know that."

"I'm sorry, Marta. But you know what I mean."

"Yeah, I guess I do. But home has people you love in it. And I don't love anybody in that place."

"What about Diana? Diana's fairly cool," Jasmine said. "I stayed there for almost a year before…" She trailed off and Kyra sensed her reluctance to finish her train of thought. Kyra knew what finishing the sentence would have led to. After leaving the group home where Marta lived now, Jasmine spent a brief time on the street as a runaway, and now she was back in the system, dealing with the aftereffects of her time on the run.

"Right," Marta said, trying to ease her friend's discomfort. "Diana's okay. But then we have to put up with geeky Gary."

"Hey, he can't be that bad," Kyra said. "Otherwise he and Diana wouldn't be running a group home."

Marta gave a one-shouldered shrug. "I guess. I still think he's weird and geeky."

"You say that about your algebra teacher and the package-delivery guy and Scott in study hall," Ashley said, sending the girls into giggles again.

"Ten-minute warning," Kyra said, trying to keep a modicum of order. It was probably a losing battle, but at least she was fulfilling her responsibilities and not dozing on the job.

Forty-five minutes later the last kid had been dropped off and Josh found himself relaxing for the first time in several hours. "Okay, so now what? Originally I thought I'd offer to take you out to dinner, but it feels like all we've done all afternoon is eat. Want to find a park and walk off some of that ice cream?"

He expected Kyra to turn him down, and was surprised when she responded quickly. "Sure. I know a park full of paths that aren't too challenging between here and my place. I'll tell you how to find it." With a few succinct directions she guided him to the parking lot bordered by tall trees that were sprouting pale green new leaves and buds.

As they got out of the car Josh realized that he hadn't thought about Kyra much before he made the offer to go for a walk. "I didn't even check to make sure you had the right kind of shoes to go walking in. Is this going to be okay?"

"Fine," she assured him. "I don't own too many pairs of shoes that I couldn't use for taking a walk. They're not all up to a strenuous hike, but there are just too many crime scenes that are in less-than-perfect places for me to invest in anything but comfortable, practical shoes."

For a moment he stood still outside the car, wondering what Kyra would look like in clothes and shoes that wouldn't be at home at a crime scene. He tried to remember if he'd ever seen her that dressed-up. Even when they'd worked together out of town, Kyra favored outfits that tended toward utility, not flash. Jeans and a sweater, like her outfit today, was often the uniform of the day, with a lab coat thrown over it when needed.

Today she looked ready to take a long walk in the park without seeming to be too casual. A little breeze teased her hair, tugging one errant lock across her cheek. Josh wished he could trace its path with his fingers, but he knew that Kyra wouldn't welcome that kind of attention in the middle of the park. So he concentrated on locking up the car and following Kyra while she pointed out a path that would be slightly challenging without being much of a strain. "After all," she told him, "I need you ready to work on solving problems tomorrow in the lab."

"You can count on it." Josh tried to keep his focus on the walk, enjoying the trees that rose above them and the birds on branches over their heads. After about a third of a mile he'd managed to match his pace to Kyra's and they walked companionably together.

"So what did you think of the movie?" she asked, her arms swinging slowly as the path rose a little. "I liked the first fifteen minutes, and it was supposed to have a message that would interest the girls without being too preaching or too juvenile. One of the guys in Wednesday night Bible study recommended it."

"It was pretty good. I have to admit that it's been a long time since I went to a family movie like that, and I was surprised to see how much animation has changed."

"I guess that means you don't play video games, either, huh? Because if you played you'd know the kind of depth that can be achieved with computer animation."

"No time, and no interest even if I had the time," Josh admitted. He thought he saw an expression of relief on Kyra's face. "I know a lot of guys own some kind of game system, but it never seemed like fun to me. Most of the games are like parts of work I'd rather not dwell on."

"I'm glad to hear you say that. Most of the games I've seen are way too violent for my taste, although I don't believe the argument that they're the cause of all of society's ills. I can think of half a dozen things that I'd be more likely to blame society's problems on."

"Such as?" Josh was interested to hear the answer, because his perception of "church people" would have had him expecting Kyra to blast video games and music.

"Let's see…the reality of evil in the world, our fallen human nature, idol worship…"

Josh had to break in. "I can go with those first two, but *idol worship?* There aren't exactly golden calves on the street corners." The discussion had gotten a little more heated, but somehow he and Kyra were still holding hands. He wasn't sure when that had started, but he liked it.

"Not literal golden calves, but plenty of things that might as well be. There're so many things we can put before God and the important things in life, and when we do that, it's idol worship. Think about it, Josh. Most people value money, prestige, power, and they buy into the world's idea that we all need more stuff and more things to keep us busy."

Kyra's eyes sparkled and Josh was so tempted to draw much closer to her. What would it be like to have her intensity focused on him? The thought nearly made him shiver. "Okay, maybe I can agree with that. I still wouldn't say that most people worship their money and power."

Kyra shrugged. The gesture was a little dismissive and it bothered Josh. He wanted her to value his opinion. "I've seen quite a few people just around the crime lab that put their work first when they have a family, or spend all their time surfing the Net or cultivating expensive hobbies. They're all traps that are easy to fall into."

Josh felt a surge of irritation. Maybe it was because he recognized himself in Kyra's condemnations and he didn't like hearing that. "It must be nice to be able to see things in that kind of black-and-white thinking. I guess it's easy to be so superior when you've had an easy life to begin with."

Kyra spun to face him and took back her hand as if she'd been scalded. Now her eyes flashed and she pulled up to her full height. "Is that what you think? That I'm acting superior? And that my life is easy?"

Yeah, it was what he thought, but it sounded awfully harsh when Kyra said it. "Not superior, exactly, I guess. But it does look to me like your life is only as hard as you make it. You've got a job you enjoy, friends who recommend movies to go to, and none of those temptations that you see the rest of us succumbing to."

Josh thought he saw the hint of tears in her eyes, and for a moment felt badly about what he'd said. Kyra didn't give him much time to think about it. "I'm ready to go home now. Will you take me back to the church lot?"

"Fine, if that's what you want." Josh knew he probably should apologize, but Kyra's reaction seemed so over the top compared to what he'd said. They walked back to the car without speaking, and Kyra got into the passenger seat looking stiff and uncomfortable. She resisted the weak attempts at conversation Josh made on the way to the church.

Once they got there he pulled up next to her car and she was out on the pavement before he even turned the ignition off. "Thank you for driving this afternoon.

I'll make sure to reimburse you for gas when I see you at work tomorrow." She closed his car door firmly before he could argue. Less than a minute later she was starting her own car without ever looking over in his direction again. Josh had a sinking feeling that when tomorrow morning came it was going to be tense sharing an office with Kyra. He couldn't blame anybody but himself, but he still couldn't quite figure out how things went sour that quickly.

FIVE

By noon Monday, Josh thought about finding a sweater to cut the chill in the office. Kyra hadn't said one word past "hello" all morning. She studiously ignored him, going about her work without a word. When she wasn't at her computer with headphones on, she was in the lab. Normally when she went back and forth from one place to another they talked about the progress she was making, or something he'd found in his research. Only now that the office was silent did Josh realize what he was missing.

He went back through their conversation the day before in his mind half a dozen times and still didn't understand why Kyra had reacted quite the way she did. Sure, he had challenged her, but no more than he had several times during the past few weeks. What was it about his words in the park that made her shut down?

Lunchtime came and went and Kyra still wasn't speaking to him. Josh ate a solitary sandwich in the complex cafeteria and went back to the office. How could he turn this around? He stared at the computer screen, absently tapping a pen on the desk. He had been going through all the right channels for days, but so far nothing had turned up that gave him a strong lead on who any of these girls had been. At that moment Kyra came into the office, putting her lab coat on the coatrack in the corner and grabbing her purse.

"Going to lunch?" Josh asked, trying again for conversation.

"Yes, I am." Kyra looked at him for a moment, and then turned toward the door.

He had an inspiration. It was time to stop being detached from this case. "Can I go into the lab and look at things?"

Kyra stopped. "I guess. Just don't touch anything."

"I won't," he said. "See you in a bit."

Kyra nodded curtly and walked out. Josh went next door to the lab and pulled on gloves, just in case he inadvertently leaned against a gurney or made contact with something. He didn't intend to touch anything, but as unhappy as Kyra was with him already, he didn't want to make things worse.

He stood over each gurney in turn, looking at the bones. The third gurney, labeled with the letter *B* had a few more identifiable remains than the other two. Josh examined them visually from the facial bones down to the end of the gurney and back again, searching for anything that might give him another clue to the identity of these girls. After standing at the head of the gurney deep in thought for a while, he walked slowly around the area, trying to look at the bones from all sides. On his second rotation he stopped, forcing himself not to touch the place that caught his attention.

This was the set of remains where Kyra said she'd found healed fractures. Even he could see irregularities in several places on the left side of the face, and he remembered discussing with Kyra the possibility that this girl had been abused.

Josh knew that child abuse didn't always get reported; families caught in the patterns of abuse kept their dark secrets any way that they could. But broken facial bones were something severe enough to draw attention to this kid, and that meant it was likely that she'd spent time in foster care.

Maybe he could narrow the search by comparing lists of missing kids who had spent time in the system. From his work so far, he knew that there was a lot of overlap on a list like that. If he wanted to get serious, he should probably check to see how many girls and young women went missing while in care seven or eight years ago.

He went back to his computer and started pulling up all the lists he'd bookmarked before. An hour later he was nearly jubilant. He'd found five names of female juveniles who'd gone missing while in foster care in that period in the two counties closest to the dump site. In another hour he'd made eight phone calls that moved him closer to knowing a name to fit this incomplete, stark set of bones in the next room.

Tracking down people willing to talk about juveniles, even those who were missing, was always difficult, but Josh knew a few tricks from his FBI work. By four in the afternoon, he'd managed to strike two of the names off the list, one because the young woman had eventually turned up alive and the other because she'd been positively identified after dying in a meth-lab explosion years after her disappearance.

That left three names, and it was time to talk to Kyra whether he wanted to or not. She looked up when he walked into the lab, but she didn't look as shocked as she often did by his sudden appearance.

He walked in slowly, making no attempts to be silent. "Hey. You told me before that you'd have at least an ethnic group on these kids by now. Any luck?"

She nodded briefly. "On two out of three. I'm not positive on A, but B appears to be African-American, and I'd be willing to say that C was probably part black and part Asian."

Josh marveled at her precision, and wanted to find out how she could be that definite. That would have to wait, because right now he really wanted to be able to take Kyra's information and bring it back to her with a successful match. "Thanks. I'll check back in another hour." Kyra seemed surprised when he left the room as quickly as he had come. But now he had a mission, one he hoped would win him a smile from Kyra again.

Seeing Kyra smile wasn't the only reason he wanted to come up with a name. Nobody deserved to die the way these young women had, left alone and denied the right kind of final resting place. Even if they were in the foster care system, somebody somewhere cared about them and wondered why they had never come home.

She should probably apologize. Kyra turned a bone over in her hand, trying to figure out whether it was Bethany's or Abigail's metacarpal. Despite what she'd said to Josh before, it was difficult to distinguish which girl each tiny bone might belong to. She was sure that this was a human hand bone and that it belonged to one of the two. Right now she was ready to just put it on one gurney or the other in frustration and move on.

She'd been distracted all day, still so hurt by Josh's comments yesterday that she didn't want to be anywhere near him. Avoiding him proved impossible with them sharing an office, so she'd basically shut down today. Kyra knew that wasn't right, but it was the best she could do. Normally when she felt hurt, going to God in prayer made things better fairly quickly. But Josh's words kept coming back to her and the hurt stayed.

Kyra knew that holding on to hurt like this wasn't healthy. Apology and forgiveness healed the one apologizing even more than the one who'd said the hurtful things in the first place. Even though Josh had hurt her with his words, she hadn't reacted well at all. Now he looked miserable and she still couldn't bring herself to really talk to him. How long was this going to go on before one of them broke the ice? Kyra wasn't sure how long she could tolerate the distance between them; she'd gotten used to sharing her office and in several ways her life with Josh.

Last night she'd gone home feeling tense and upset. Ranger tried to lift her spirits, sitting in her lap and patting the tears off her face with a sable paw. She'd buried her face in his soft fur and let the pain wash over her. There was so much that Josh didn't know about her, and what had happened in her life, but she wasn't ready to tell him. No one around her knew what her early life had been like, and the last thing she wanted from Josh was pity.

In her musing Kyra realized that she'd placed several small bones without even thinking about it. She checked each gurney carefully, but nothing looked out of place. Even in her distraction she was doing her job the way it was supposed to be done. She breathed a quick prayer of thanks that God's care surrounded her even when she wasn't too aware of it. The thought brought a brief smile to her face that spread even broader when Josh burst through the door with papers in his hand.

"Serita Waldron," he said smugly, putting the papers down on the end of gurney B. It took a moment for Kyra to figure out what he meant. Then she looked down at the slightly fuzzy faxes in front of her with a picture of a serious girl with large eyes and a slightly defiant expression.

"Serita Waldron," she echoed, tracing the picture with a finger, touching the line of the girl's left cheekbone where a slight imperfection made an indentation. The same fault was obvious in the facial bones on this gurney. Thanks to Josh this girl had a name, perhaps even a family somewhere.

"Okay, tell me all about it," she said to him, watching his smile spread.

"I remembered what you said about the likelihood of this girl being in the foster care system. I'd already found at least ten missing girls and women that fit that category. Just on a chance I decided to narrow things down a little and look at the ones who were still in the system at the time they went missing."

"That was taking a chance, wasn't it?"

Josh shrugged. "If I was wrong, I figured I could always expand my search again. Narrowing it to girls and women who went missing in care, I got five names. Two of those I ruled out because they'd been identified one way or another."

Kyra tried not to wince, knowing that the way Josh phrased that meant that at least one of them was dead. "Okay, go on."

"Once you told me that the bones probably belonged to an African-American, one of my possibilities faded because she was Latina. When I pulled as many records as I could on the two remaining possibilities, I knew it had to be Serita. Even to my untrained eye, the contour of the face matched."

They both looked down at the fax on the gurney, near the reconstructed left cheekbone. "This is good. With one of them identified, maybe we'll have an easier time with the other two."

"But all you have is still two gurneys of bones, and not that many bones. Do you think that's possible?"

"You probably know about as much about serial

killers as I do. They have patterns and routines. Something will connect these three. We can almost count on it."

"At least we've got a start." Josh didn't move, but he had a more serious expression now. "Does this mean we'll keep talking? Even if it's just to work on the case. I can't stand being this close and not talking."

Kyra felt surprised at how deeply she reacted to his admission. "Me, neither. We'll keep talking. For now it will be about the case, but maybe we can branch out again in a few days."

His answering smile was brief. "I'd like that. Until I put my foot in my mouth yesterday it was a very good day. I'd like to find a way to get back to the place we were before about five yesterday afternoon."

Kyra found herself stiffening. "I don't think that's possible. Maybe we can move forward to a place where we can be friends again, though. Will that work?"

"I'll make it work." Josh's pale blue eyes made a silent promise that he meant every word he said. With that kind of determination, Kyra thought, if Josh wanted to be more than friends he might find a way.

For the next three days, Josh found himself working as hard as Kyra. As she tried to match every last bone they had recovered to one of the three gurneys, he investigated every possible connection that the other two young women might have to Serita Waldron. Whoever the young woman was whose remains were on gurney A, she was proving the most elusive. Unlike the other two, she didn't have any distinguishing features to her bones. At least with the remains on gurney C they knew they were looking for someone who'd given birth at a young age.

Late Thursday afternoon Josh went into the lab to tell Kyra he was leaving for the day. He'd hit one dead end too many in the past nine hours, and it was time to go home for a while. Most of his body hurt from concentrating on the task of identifying the murder victims. His back and neck ached from hours at the computer, and a tension headache made his temples throb and his muscles tense.

Almost all of that evaporated when he walked into the lab and found Kyra at work. She had her back to him and the droop in her shoulders made Josh think she felt as discouraged as he did. Instead of giving up, though, Kyra was leaning over gurney A in a posture he'd come to recognize as prayer. She was praying over the bones as she worked, and he suspected she was asking for help in her task. It touched him deeply to think of her doing this. Her slender hands spread out over the steel of the gurney, and her hair fanned over the collar of her lab coat.

"Hey, there," she said softly. "I'm not turning around, but I can hear you, Josh. Am I getting used to the quiet way you walk or have you been making an effort to be louder so you don't startle me?"

"A little bit of both, I think." Josh didn't want to admit that he'd been extremely deliberate in his movements when he went into the lab, trying to make just a little noise in order not to scare her. "You call her Abigail, don't you?"

She turned toward him, away from the gurney. Her green eyes were wide and a tiny line creased her brow. "Yes, but how did you know that? It's not exactly common knowledge."

"I heard you talking to Allie the other day," he admitted.

She seemed to blush a little. "You probably think I'm a little bit crazy."

"No, not at all. I think it's a good thing to do. A name makes us all look at things a different way. This isn't just an unknown body that's been out in the elements for years, it's a young woman whose family would probably want to come visit her if they could."

Kyra appeared to do a double take. "Yes, that's exactly how I feel, but I didn't think..."

"That you'd ever hear me say that? I wouldn't have a couple of weeks ago. But working here with you, I've come to see things your way. Not everything," he added quickly. "But I agree with you on this issue."

She smiled a slow and tentative smile that gave his heart a jump. "I know you still don't agree with the way I feel about God, but seeing each person as valuable is a good first step."

"It may be the only step in that direction that I ever take."

Kyra was still smiling. "I don't know. I suspect you might surprise yourself in that respect. We'll just have to see about that, won't we?"

"We will," he agreed. "But for now I'm going home. I'm tired, hungry and I feel sore all over."

"I can understand all of that. It's the way I feel, too." She was silent for a minute, and then turned toward him. "If you give me about fifteen minutes to close down here, I'll offer to take you home for dinner."

"That would be great," Josh said, wondering what to say next. "While you get things done here, I'll run one small errand and meet you there."

"Okay. But don't you need me to tell you where I live first?"

Now Josh felt himself turning red. "Yeah, I guess I do." He'd been so glad that she'd asked, yet so focused on what he had to do before he got there, that he'd forgotten that little point. "Tell me what I can bring."

Kyra waved him away. "Just yourself. This isn't going to be fancy. I put stuff for soup in the slow cooker this morning and there's plenty for two."

"All right." Kyra gave him directions to her house and he jotted them down so he wouldn't get lost. He was still learning parts of this corner of Maryland, so far from his haunts around D.C. Until now there hadn't been much to draw him out to this area.

His errand didn't take long; he went to a local pharmacy for antihistamines. If he was going to hang out with Kyra's feline housemate without sneezing his head off, he needed to medicate beforehand.

Kyra's house was small but comfortable. It looked like a sixties tract home that had seen a lot of renovation. Her kitchen table was oak, with a smooth top that Josh imagined had seen thousands of meals. "Did you refinish this yourself?" He ran a hand over the golden surface.

"The last time, yes. It was my grandmother's table, and I know she and Gramps redid it at least once themselves. But that was before I was old enough to remember anything like that. By the time I was seven she was a widow. Ranger, no!"

Kyra was fussing at the cat, who'd plumped his heavy black body on Josh's lap and was busy rubbing the side of his head on Josh's shirt buttons. He was glad he'd taken that antihistamine; cats had a way of sensing his discomfort and heading for him instinctively. "Come on, cat. You don't really want to sit on me."

The cat disagreed, settling in and actually purring. Kyra came over and picked up the animal, who protested just a little. "I should have fed him the minute I got home. That way he would have left us alone. But I wanted to tidy up a little before you got here. You didn't need to see the four pairs of shoes in my living room."

"Probably not. I wouldn't even have known about them if you hadn't told me. I could have imagined that you're just a terribly neat individual."

"That would be imagination, all right." Kyra went across the open space and deposited Ranger on the raised hearth of the family room fireplace, where two small dishes sat. Before he could complain she opened a large tin and poured out dry cat kibble. Ranger settled down to his dinner and Kyra came back to the kitchen, washed her hands and set about serving their meal.

"I'd ask you to say grace, but I don't want to embarrass you," she said as she sat down a few minutes later. Instead, she said a brief simple blessing over the steaming soup and passed Josh the bread basket.

They ate in silence for a few minutes, the only sound being Ranger across the room crunching on cat food. Finally Josh spoke up. "This is great. You may not think it's fancy, but it's really good soup. At my place soup comes out of a can."

Kyra laughed a little. "Not here. I take a few short-cuts, but that isn't one of them. I might use frozen vegetables or store-bought stock, but real beef and barley and mushrooms went in there, too."

"And you did a good job. In fact, I'd like another bowl if you don't mind."

"Not at all." Kyra took his bowl and dished up more soup. "It's nice to see my cooking appreciated."

Josh felt like telling her that he appreciated much more than her cooking, but he didn't want that to be taken the wrong way, so he said nothing. He was saved from getting into trouble by the cat, who started weaving around one of his ankles, meowing loudly.

"You're not getting any soup, not from Josh and not from me," Kyra said, looking down at the cat. She watched the animal for a while, then took her attention from Ranger to Josh. "Are you allergic to cats?"

"And dogs. What did I do to give myself away?"

"Nothing," she said. "It just seems to be part of life that cats pay the most attention to people who would rather not have them around."

Josh shrugged. "For a cat, he's okay. And the antihistamine I took before I came seems to be working, so I don't mind the attention too much."

"Maybe we can keep being friends after all," Kyra said softly, leaving Josh wondering exactly what she meant. He was still wondering when he drove home that night, seeing the image of Kyra's sparkling green eyes as he thought about her words.

SIX

"Ranger says hi," Kyra said as she dropped her things on the desk Friday. Josh grimaced slightly but didn't turn around from his focus on the computer screen.

"Did he send anything with his greetings? A catnip mouse or a hairball?"

"No, but I'll make sure that you get the next one he's ready to give away." She went over to the coffeepot and poured a mug of the steaming liquid that had just finished brewing. "You're in early this morning."

"Yeah, well, I had an idea that woke me up in the middle of the night, so I came in to check it out. I might have a possible identity for Chloe."

Kyra felt a chill go up her spine. "That's great. Tell me about it."

"I got to thinking about one of the guidelines we've been using to determine age, and it reminded me of my sister."

She was tempted to break in and say that she didn't know Josh had a sister, but Kyra kept the statement to herself. He wouldn't appreciate anything that led away from the point he was trying to make. She nodded in encouragement.

"I know you said that most people have their wisdom teeth by eighteen, but not everybody does. My sister was twenty-three before she had the surgery to remove hers that were impacted. That made me think that maybe I had narrowed the field a little too much."

"So you went up a couple of years on the age of the young women you were looking at?"

"Just a little bit. And that led me to Gen Bailey. Gen disappeared shortly after she aged out of the foster care system, leaving behind a two-year-old son, Andre."

Josh typed on his laptop for a moment and pulled up a picture on the screen. Kyra looked over his shoulder to see a smiling young woman holding a toddler with dark hair and even darker wide eyes. "Gen's mother was Vietnamese, her father African-American, and both had some major drug problems. Her dad went to prison and died there, and her mom abandoned her by the time she was six. She bounced around the system a lot, with her last placement being a group home for teen girls and their children."

Kyra felt a tension in her spine. "What happened to Andre once his mom disappeared?"

"His father was tracked down, and his grandmother is raising him. He's almost nine years old now."

"Does he still live in the area?"

"He and his grandmother live in Baltimore. I'm not sure about the father. He doesn't appear to be in the state prison system, at least. Do you think we can talk the grandmother into letting us take a DNA sample from Andre?"

"Probably, especially if it means we can tell her what happened to Andre's mom. We haven't had too many people turn us down in situations like this." Kyra looked at him, still at the computer. "If I call her and she says yes, do you want to come with me to get the sample?"

"Yes. Let me know when. I can even drive if you like. I think my car might look a little more official than your pickup." He smiled and Kyra found herself smiling back, because he was probably right.

Three days later when they pulled up in front of the brick row house in the city of Baltimore, Kyra was sure that Josh had been right. The pickup truck would not have looked as official as his car. The sedan Josh drove looked as if it could be FBI issue—sedate and nondescript. It served well for an errand like this, though.

Kyra noticed that Josh himself looked like an FBI agent today, in his dark suit, pale blue shirt and sedate tie. He let her go ahead, ringing the bell and waiting for an answer. In a few minutes a small woman with dark skin and espresso-colored hair flecked with silver opened the door. "Mrs. Quinn? I'm Dr. Elliott, we spoke on the phone."

The woman eyed her warily. "I'd like to see some identification. You hardly look old enough to be a doctor of anything."

Kyra felt like telling the woman that she hardly looked old enough to have a grandson in third grade herself, but she was used to doubts about her official status, so she merely reached into her purse and pulled out an ID wallet.

Mrs. Quinn looked it over carefully before she closed it and handed it back. "Thank you. I always tell Andre that you just can't be too careful, so I better practice what I preach to the child." She tilted her head to see around Kyra. "And who's your partner here? Another doctor?"

"No, I'm just an investigator." Josh held out his own identification. "Joshua Richards, on loan from the FBI."

Mrs. Quinn pressed her thin lips together into a thinner line. "If you think that's going to impress me, you have another thing coming. But I don't want you just standing out here on the stoop, so I better get you inside."

The inside of the brownstone was as neat as the outside. The furniture was slightly worn, but everything was clean. "Andre should be home from school soon. I told him there was going to be someone coming to get a sample from him and I told him it wouldn't hurt. I hope I was right."

Kyra was glad that she didn't have to tell this intense woman that she planned to hurt her grandson. "You were right. All we'll do is swab the inside of his cheek. We'll take the sample back to the lab and see if his DNA is related to the unidentified woman we have."

"I almost hope it is. It's hard on a child when nobody can tell him where his mama went. I only met her twice, but Gen didn't seem to be the kind of person who would walk out on her son."

She gestured toward a framed photo on top of a bookcase. It was the same shot that Josh had pulled up on the computer; perhaps the only one of Gen and Andre taken together, Kyra thought. Next to it were several smaller photos that were obviously school pictures of an older version of the toddler on Gen's lap. The chubby cheeks of the baby gave way to a slender, solemn face with the same dark eyes looking out past the focus of the camera. Kyra felt compassion for the little boy being raised by his grandmother, wondering about his mother.

"What about his father?" she found herself asking.

"He's around some. Not as often as I'd like him to be. I keep telling Deon that he's nearly thirty, with a child to raise, and he needs to settle down and be the one to raise him." Her resolute expression told Kyra that apparently her son didn't always listen to what his mother had to say.

"What does your son do for a living, Mrs. Quinn?" It was the first time Josh had spoken since introducing himself. Kyra had almost forgotten he was there with them. She knew that he'd been taking in the room in a different way than she had, and she was anxious to hear what he had to say about his perceptions.

"He's a security guard in a mall during the daytime, and goes to community college at night. He had his wild days when he was younger, but that's over with now." Kyra wondered whether the woman believed what she was saying. There was a hesitancy in her voice, as if she was trying to convince herself.

"If he's a security guard his wilder days can't have been too wild," Josh said. "What's he studying?"

"Administration of justice. He's always been interested in being a policeman. I think it's a dangerous job for somebody with a child, but Deon doesn't see it that way. And he says he can't be around more because he's got to get into the academy soon or he'll be too old."

"He has a point there," Kyra conceded. Before she could say anything else, she heard a school bus pull to a stop somewhere close outside with a whoosh of brakes. In a few moments the front door opened and closed.

"Hey, Grandma. Are the people here? The ones from the crime lab?" There was a thump in the hall behind them and a young boy appeared.

"Take off your shoes before you come in here," Mrs. Quinn cautioned her grandson. "I don't want muddy prints everyplace. Then come in and say hello to our guests."

He nodded and headed swiftly back to the front door, and now Kyra could hear two smaller thumps that made her grin as she identified them as the thud on a hardwood floor of two heavy tennis shoes. Sliding a little in sock feet, Andre came back to the living room. "Chris at school said that they'd probably cut a big ol' chunk of my hair off for the sample, and maybe poke me to get blood." He eyed Kyra and Josh suspiciously, waiting to hear what they said in return.

"Chris at school has been watching too much TV," Josh said. He lowered himself to third-grade level as Andre came closer. "And he hasn't even been watching the good shows. You can go back to school and tell Chris that we don't need to stick you to get blood, and nobody cuts your hair unless Grandma says it's too long." That drew a brief smile from the child. Josh might have said he didn't know much about teenagers, but younger boys he was okay with.

"All we're going to do is what's called a buccal swab, Andre. You open your mouth good and wide, and we rub the inside of your cheek. Some cells rub off on the swab and we take them back to the lab and run tests on them."

The child still looked suspicious. "Hey, you get to stick your tongue out at a grown-up without getting into trouble," Josh told him, prompting a grin. "And if you're worried about it hurting or anything, I'll do it first. That way we can both stick our tongues out at Dr. Elliott, what do you say?"

"Okay." Kyra got her supplies out of her kit, and Josh counted to three. Then he and Andre both stuck their tongues out and Kyra took swabs from both of them.

"You can close your mouth now," she told Andre a moment later. "And you did a very good job. Thank you for being so cooperative." He smiled at her and watched while she labeled the containers for the swabs, writing their names on the sides of the vials.

"How long will it be before you get results?" Andre's grandmother asked. "I have to expect that part of the television shows is wrong, too. They couldn't wrap things up neatly in forty-five minutes unless they got instant results, could they?"

"You're right, Mrs. Quinn. DNA testing isn't usually an overnight process. We might have some news in about a week. I'll make sure that you know as soon as we do."

"Thank you, Dr. Elliott. After more than seven years, I guess we can wait one more week."

Kyra packed up and Mrs. Quinn showed them out of the house. "You did a good job in there," she told Josh as they got into his car. "Despite what you've said about not being good with teens, you seemed to have a real knack with Andre."

Josh shrugged. "Yeah. I remember being his age and wishing that grown-ups would explain things to me. When I was ten and my dad died, nobody ever answered my questions or tried to help me understand the situation. I decided then that not only was I going to find out the truth about my father, but I wouldn't ever treat a kid the way I had been treated then."

"Wow. That was a lot more information than I expected," Kyra said. It made a lot of sense, though, and gave her a whole different view of Josh. "I remember you said one time that you had a sister. Older or younger?"

She was pretty sure that she knew the answer to that one but wanted to hear it from him. "Younger," he says. "Three years younger, which means she was seven when our dad died and I was ten."

"That kind of explains why you're better at handling little boys than teenage girls. You just don't have any experience with them, do you?"

He shook his head. "I don't. By the time my sister

was a teenager I had pretty much left home. We lived with my grandparents by then and I had a scholarship to college that didn't cover trips home to Iowa."

"What happened to your mom? Did she remarry?" The question was out before Kyra could check herself.

"She…died." He was silent for a moment and Kyra felt sorry that she'd asked. Then his eyes flashed with a glint like steel. "I might as well be honest. She killed herself when I was fourteen and my sister was eleven. She couldn't handle the shame anymore."

He turned and looked out the window, then started the car and started driving away while Kyra wanted to ask many more questions, but feeling at the same time that she'd already asked way too much.

Josh scanned the screen of his computer again, hoping that he had missed something, that there was a piece of information that he hadn't found before. The third un-identified girl was still a mystery with no solution. The bones just weren't yielding their secrets either for Kyra or for him, or any of the other people in the lab.

"Come on, who are you?" he muttered, looking through the faces again. He'd called up virtually every missing girl from twelve to eighteen, in the foster care system or out, and still there was no way to tell who she was. Kyra still couldn't say for sure what her background was because there were few pieces of the skull or other markers for ethnicity or other identification. There were no broken and healed bones, and the girl's projected height of five foot four put her squarely at average.

Even with no help in figuring out who she was, Josh still wanted to be the one to discover her identity. He knew that Kyra called her Abigail, the last of the three to still have her real name unknown to them. Surely she had something in common with Serita and Gen. Of course, Gen's identity wasn't for sure yet, but Kyra was fairly certain that the DNA tests would verify that the missing young woman was Andre's mother. Given her experience, Josh was willing to trust her opinion on the matter.

It was disheartening to think that perhaps Abigail might forever remain a Jane Doe. Josh decided to run a narrower search pattern again and see how many possible matches he came up with. Instead of keeping a lot of variables, this time he concentrated on those who had gone missing from foster care from just two counties in a time frame overlapping Serita's and Gen's disappearances and eighteen months earlier.

Doing that yielded only six possibilities instead of the fifteen or more he'd had with a broader search. Josh went through the in-depth information on the six, looking for links with the other two. Three of the six had attended the same schools as both known victims. Two had definitely used the same medical clinic as Gen. Several of the six had been housed in the same private homes, group homes or centers as both Gen or Serita, although none at the same time as the two who'd already been identified.

"Any luck? You've sure been focused on that," Kyra said, making him jump slightly in his chair.

"I guess you're right. I didn't even hear you come up behind me," he told her, looking over his shoulder.

She smiled, looking even more youthful than usual. "Good. Maybe I'm learning the technique from you, Josh. I'm usually the one somebody has to scrape off the ceiling because you snuck up on me."

"Guess you have a point there." He opened several windows on his computer and pointed to the different pieces of information he'd found regarding some of the missing young women. "Nothing is pointing me in one person's direction, but I've narrowed it to six that have more than one thing in common with Gen or Serita."

"Hey, that's a good start. Where do you go from here? Normally I focus on forensics, rather than talking to people, so I have no idea how your end of the investigation works."

Josh thought she might have been exaggerating a little to make him feel more adept. He decided to put aside his minor doubts and take her at face value. "Now I hit the streets for a day or two and see if I can get any information that isn't in these profiles. I'll figure out if we can narrow this list of six down. Some of them may have shown up…one way or another."

Josh could almost feel Kyra's flash of pain when she took in his meaning. "I hope if any of them have shown up, it's alive."

"I hope so, too, but it's not always the case." He sent the six profile sheets to the printer and shut down his computer. "I'll let you know what I find."

"Do that. And Josh? Please, be careful while you're checking this out."

This time he was the one feeling the pain. How long had it been since anybody cared whether or not he was careful about anything? All he could do was nod before he went to get his sheets from the printer. If he said anything, Kyra would hear the catch in his voice and he didn't want that.

Twenty-four hours later Josh was down to five possible victims. Kyra would be happy to hear that the sixth had turned up alive, but no one had ever pulled her missing persons report. Now he stood in a medical clinic office and watched one of the techs work.

There was something about the guy that bothered Josh. Normally he could figure out what bugged him about a suspect right away, but so far what he felt was a vague unease he couldn't define. The man looked to be in his mid-thirties; his height and build were both so average as to make him nondescript. He had olive skin and short brown hair and close-set eyes. All in all Josh thought he had so few distinguishing features that he could have been invisible.

Every ten minutes or so he called another name and someone would follow him back into an area that appeared to be a testing lab. Josh tried to keep himself from jumping to conclusions, but the guy wasn't helping him any. The med tech's demeanor was blunt and impatient, and Josh noticed he didn't make small talk with any of the patients whose names he called. It was kind of like watching some kind of android work, except androids probably didn't have smirks like this guy.

Before Josh could get up and talk to the tech, someone else called his name and he found himself ushered into the office of the clinic manager. "You realize that I can't tell you much regarding patients here. Government regulations won't let us release much information without a warrant." Her thin aquiline nose seemed to turn up in distaste as she talked to Josh, and the corner of her mouth curled in displeasure.

"I understand that, but what I'm asking for is legal." Josh tried to give her a winning smile, but he felt out of practice and his efforts were wasted on the woman. "We already know through other sources that two people whose bodies we've identified were patients at this clinic shortly before they disappeared. Now I've got one more unidentified young woman and at least five different possibilities for who she is."

"And you expect me to help you with that?" Her voice was flat.

Josh spread out the five sheets he'd printed out. "As much as you can. All I'm asking of you is to check and see if any of these names show activity as patients after the date they were reported missing." He put up a hand before she could open her mouth in protest. "And before you say anything, I'm an FBI special agent and I know that the tougher medical privacy laws enacted in the past few years aren't retroactive."

Her sour expression told him that she hadn't expected him to know that. "Come back tomorrow morning before ten and I'll see what I can do."

"I'll be in at eight-forty-five," Josh told her, making a mental note to be there at eight-forty at the latest and wondering what he could do then to put her in a better mood. The woman reminded him so much of his sixth-grade English teacher that he doubted that a good mood was a possibility. He couldn't think of a single thing he could bring in the morning that might put a smile on this woman's face.

SEVEN

Who was this guy, and what was he doing? The Watcher had seen him twice now, and had gotten a bad feeling both times. He looked too sharp, and everything about him screamed *cop*. The last thing he needed right now was some kind of investigator getting close to him. First they'd ruined his garden and now there had been an article buried back in the paper about a skeleton being identified as a kid who'd gone missing seven years ago.

The Watcher felt like pacing, but right now he couldn't afford to draw attention to himself, especially not with this guy around. It was bad enough that woman from the crime lab was nosing around. Now she had some kind of investigator working for her, and they'd gotten way too close to suit him. He was having a hard time controlling the urges now, and the girls were getting bolder. Yesterday one of them had stared at him as if daring him to take her on. *Soon, he thought. It's going to happen soon.* Now, what could he do to get these two nuisances out of the way first?

Whatever idea he came up with, it would have to be subtle and quiet. His life right now was set up the way he liked it. He had a decent job, relationships he was happy with, and he didn't want to mess that up. As long as the girls stopped staring at him he'd be okay.

"You were right," Josh said in a near whisper. Kyra nudged him with her elbow, making him stop talking before the beaming clinic manager got close enough to hear him.

He hadn't believed her when she'd told him what to take to the clinic as a present if he wanted the manager to smile at him. "Paper towels? I was thinking a rose, or coffee, or chocolate or something."

"Trust me on this one," she'd told him. "Clinics that run on a shoestring never have enough supplies of any kind. Coffee won't thrill her nearly as much as a box of file folders or the paper goods they most likely go through with lightning speed." His wary look last night had told her that he didn't think she was right, but when they'd gotten in his car this morning, there was a twenty-four-roll pack of paper towels in the backseat.

"Bringing gifts and right on time," the manager said, sitting down at her desk and not looking at all like the unhappy person Josh had described yesterday. Kyra tried mightily not to look smug, merely smiling back at the woman and not even thinking *I told you so.*

"Gifts and my boss," Josh said, rising to greet the clinic manager. "This is Dr. Elliott from the state forensics lab. She's the one who is in charge of the department that's identified Gen and Serita."

"Were you the clinic manager that long ago, Ms. Underwood?" Kyra was pretty sure of what the woman's answer would be, but part of it caught her off guard, anyway.

"Not the manager, but I did work here," she said as they all sat down in the chairs around her battered desk. "I'm an RN, and back then I was running parenting classes and some other programs. I remember Gen and her son. I was so surprised when she stopped coming to the clinic because she really seemed to care about that child."

"She did," Kyra said, feeling sorrow creep up on her. She willed herself not to cry and instead focused on the metal surface of the desk.

"I would think there would be a high turnover in a clinic," Josh said, saving her from showing how choked her voice had become. "Besides you, are there any employees that have stayed that long?"

"Dr. Perry has been here for ten years. I think he's planned on retiring the whole time and just can't bring himself to do it, because he knows how hard we'll have to look to replace him. And the ultrasound and X-ray clinician, Ramon Garcia, has been with us that long, I think."

Kyra saw Josh lean forward just a little, and his eyes lit up. He'd told her last night about his feelings regarding the man he pointed out in the lobby when they arrived this morning. Kyra tried to keep her own opinions to herself, but if Josh pressed her she'd be forced to admit that there seemed to be something a little "off" about the man.

"Would I have seen Mr. Garcia in the waiting room yesterday?"

"Probably. We don't have enough staff to give him someone to call his patients in for testing, so he does that himself." Ms. Underwood looked down at the file folder she had brought to the desk with her when she met them. "But you were asking last night about these five women. I can't tell you much, but I do have some information for you."

"We'll be happy to take what you can give us." Now Kyra was the one leaning forward, praying silently that maybe now they could identify the third victim.

"I found something on three of them. I'm afraid that in one case it isn't good news, but it removed Amy from your possible victims. Apparently she committed suicide five years ago."

Kyra's heart sank. "I'm sorry to hear that. And the other two?"

"Better, at least a little bit. Maria turned up in Texas under a different name and Jade was referred by our clinic to a battered woman's shelter just three years ago. So that leaves two of your original five still unaccounted for."

"And both of these two were in the foster care system at the time of their disappearance," Josh said, a rising note in his voice. "Thank you, Ms. Underwood. You've been very helpful."

The woman seemed to do a slight double take. "You're welcome. Does this mean you're not going to press me for information on these two?" She held out the information sheets on the remaining young women.

"If we need to, we can get a warrant so that you won't be in a compromising situation," Josh said. "You've done what you can legally and I truly appreciate it. Why should I push it?"

Ms. Underwood looked over at Kyra. "Yesterday Mr. Richards told me he was from the FBI. Was he putting me on? I've never met a federal agent even halfway this pleasant."

"He's a rarity," Kyra said. As she got to know Josh more with every passing week, she was discovering just how unusual he really was. And in almost every way, unusual was good. On the way back to the office she wanted to find a way to tell him, but she couldn't think of a way that sounded right with somebody that they had both agreed was just a colleague, a friend.

"I still don't like the way Garcia looks at his patients," Josh said at a stoplight. "But that's not enough to check to see if he has a record."

Kyra sighed. She didn't want to admit that she wasn't all that fond of the technician's expression, either. "No, it isn't. And we have work to do to see if the bones we're calling Abigail could be either of those missing young women."

Josh grimaced. "I don't know whether to hope that it is or that it isn't. The truth is that those bones belong to someone, and if we know who she is, she'll eventually get a decent burial and any family she might have will know what happened to her."

Kyra sat back in her seat, even more surprised than she was in the clinic manager's office. This was a whole different attitude than Joshua would have expressed a few weeks ago. She breathed a silent prayer of thanks as they pulled into the parking lot of the lab and she got ready to go to work.

Several times in the next few days Josh surprised her with his compassionate attitude. There was still no definitive piece of evidence that told them who the last body belonged to. What they did have pointed to the girl either being Lisa Phipps or Nikki Carter. One had been thirteen when she disappeared, the other fifteen. After more than seven years there was little left of either child's existence to try to figure out which one it might be.

Kyra looked at the information they had on the two, searching one more time to see what they could have missed. One thing nagged at her from the information sheets—what was it? Both had gone to the medical clinic she and Josh had checked out. Each had disappeared while they were still in the foster care system. Lisa had a father living at the time of her disappearance, but he'd been in state prison serving time for killing her mother. Nikki had been in foster care since shortly after her eighth birthday, bouncing through several placements.

Nikki's longest stay was at the group home where Marta lived right now. Kyra tried to think about what the girls had said about the home on their last movie date. In a few moments it came to her; the group home parents, Diana and Gary Griffith were still the same ones who'd been there seven years ago and even a few years earlier than that. Marta had said Diana was "okay," which was grudging praise for her.

Kyra wondered if Diana was the kind of foster parent who saved something from every child whose life she shared. If Kyra was fortunate, she would be. It wouldn't take much to say whether or not their missing girl was Nikki. "Time for another trip out in the field," she told Josh as she entered her office. "This time I want to be the one who gets the last piece of the puzzle."

"Fine with me," Josh said. "As long as I don't have to work with bones while you're out investigating, I'm good."

"Don't worry, I wouldn't do that to you," Kyra said, suppressing the laugh that threatened at the mental image of Josh in the lab. "In fact, why don't I give you the information on Lisa's father and have you and Terry go out to the state prison where he's housed and collect a sample so that we can clear the identity of this body one way or another?"

"Okay. Where are we going?" Josh didn't look thrilled, but he wasn't arguing, either.

Kyra looked down at her information. "Cumberland. It's about a hundred-and-twenty-five miles from here. If you two get going in the next hour, you can be back here before rush hour this evening."

"Great. Do you want to tell Terry or shall I?"

"I'll do it," Kyra said. She wondered what on earth the two men would talk about for six hours or more together in a car. Maybe, she hoped, they would find a shared interest in the same kind of music, or sports radio or something. In any case, she'd picked the best assignment for herself this time.

"She'd be twenty-one now." Nate Phipps spoke quietly, more thoughtful than Josh expected him to be. He had the pallor of someone who'd spent nearly fifteen years in a maximum-security prison, and the physique of a man who spent many hours working out. His short hair was sprinkled with gray that Josh knew hadn't been there when he started his sentence, and there were creases around his eyes that had never come from smiling.

"Who, your daughter?" Terry said, storing the buccal swab in its tube after swabbing the inside of Phipps's cheek and carefully labeling it before storing everything in a heavy plastic zipper bag.

"Yeah, Lisa. She was five when I went in here. I wouldn't be able to recognize her today if she walked by. And don't call her my daughter. That's what me and Dani fought about."

Josh couldn't believe that the man could sit here that calmly and discuss his wife's murder, even if it had happened so many years before. It explained why Phipps hadn't argued any about giving them his DNA; he didn't think it would tell them anything even if the bones they had were Lisa's.

"So you didn't think she was yours?" Josh tried not to let the contempt show in his voice. Apparently he didn't do a very good job of it if the man's expression was any indication. Twin grooves furrowed his heavy brows as he scowled.

"No, I didn't think she was mine. She didn't look anything like my family. Even the women in my family are big-boned, strong with dark hair. Lisa, she looked just like her mother, a little thing with pale hair. And she was sick all the time."

Josh could see Terry open his mouth as if he was going to argue with the prisoner. He shot the technician a look to try to tell him to let the subject alone. Either Terry understood him or he came to the same conclusion on his own, because he shrugged but stayed silent. "We'll let you know what we find out in a couple of weeks, Mr. Phipps," Josh told him.

"I already know what you're going to find," the con said in a flat voice. "No matter what, that isn't my kid down in Pikesville. End of story." He must have meant what he said, because even though the man was shackled to the metal table in the small room, Josh could see Phipps try to get up to signal the guard.

"We can do that for you," Terry said, his lips pressed in a thin, cold line. He seemed to want to get out of the prisoner's presence even more quickly than Phipps wanted to leave them. Josh knocked on the door and they exited, letting the guard know that Phipps wanted to go back to his cell.

"Guys like that leave a bad taste in my mouth,"

Terry said later in the prison's parking lot. "How about we pick up some food for the road, and a strong coffee? It's another two or three hours back to the lab."

"Sure." Josh didn't know what else to say. He wasn't all that hungry, but the idea of coffee sounded good. Besides, he needed something to keep him awake on the trip other than Terry's chatter. One more sentence about fantasy sports leagues and he'd be tempted to leave the tech by the side of the road.

When he got back to the lab, he tried to slip in quietly and do what he needed to do without having to talk to anybody, but it didn't work. Kyra sat at her desk, musing over something on the desk.

"Hi," she said, looking up. "I hate to even ask how your trip was."

"I look that good, huh?" Josh felt impressed by her insight from just one look at him.

"Hey, I sent you to the state prison. That in itself can't be good. And I have to think that Phipps wasn't just a swell guy or he wouldn't be in there."

"Was your afternoon better?"

"I think so. Diane is the best kind of foster parent. She has something of every kid that's ever been with them, both in her heart and with a few real mementos as well."

"So she kept things from Nikki, then?"

"Yes. More than usual because she said Nikki was special somehow. She left hurriedly to go someplace else, and left a lot of her stuff behind."

When Kyra looked up at him, her eyes were moist with tears. "Diane called it a lot of stuff, but it was a pretty small pile to represent all of somebody's worldly goods. We got lucky, though. One of the things she left was a hairbrush." She held up a clear bag with a pink plastic brush. "It was in a shoe box, protected all this time. We should be able to extract enough DNA from the hair to see if it's Nikki on the gurney."

"Good. According to Phipps, we won't find out anything from his DNA. He claims to be sure that Lisa wasn't his daughter."

"Ouch. Is that what made you look beat up around the edges?"

The words were on the tip of his tongue to deny what Kyra said, but Josh stopped himself, thinking. "Yes, I think it is. Hearing him say that just brought back bad memories from my own childhood. After my dad died when I was ten, I spent five years hearing what a rotten human being people thought he was."

He took a deep, ragged breath, feeling the story come out of him like something rushing out of a cage. "My mother moved us away from Chicago back to her hometown where nobody had heard about all the allegations against him, how he'd been a corrupt U.S. marshal who'd killed himself in disgrace. I never thought it was true, but if I dared say that, we'd get into arguments that would last for hours."

"Last week you told me your mom killed herself because she couldn't live with the shame of something. Was this why?"

Josh felt tears sting behind his eyelids, and looked down at the floor while he nodded. "Somehow,

Chrissie, my sister, always blamed me for her death. She said if I hadn't brought our father's name up so often, she wouldn't have been reminded. I sent Chrissie everything once the people who framed my father for their own crimes had been arrested and convicted. I thought maybe she'd call me or write me and apologize or something."

"Didn't she say anything?" Kyra's voice sounded small and surprised. Josh wasn't sure when she'd gotten up out of her chair to come and stand beside him. Now she put a hand on his arm. He didn't push her away.

"I got a birthday card two months later. And at Christmas the same photo card as usual, she and her perfect family all dressed up in their red-and-green plaid, even a bow of it on the dog. No note, just the card."

"Awww…" Kyra said, the tone in her voice saying more than a full sentence would have. Her arms were around him and she leaned against him. Josh buried his face in her dark auburn hair, trying to memorize the earthy floral scent of her shampoo. She felt so good, so accepting, and he wondered if this was anything like how God's love felt to Kyra. It if was, he could see why she was so calm and peaceful most of the time.

"Can you teach me how to do that?" he asked, his voice cracking slightly.

"Do what?" Her eyes held puzzlement.

"Love somebody, act as if you don't care who they are or what they've done but still love them, anyway?"

She looked up at him, seeming to search his face for

several long moments. "I can try," she told him. "But I'm pretty sure it's a God thing. Think you can handle that?"

He leaned farther into her embrace, the wonderful scent of her. "Let's see. All I know is that I want what you've got, and if that comes from God then maybe I'll have to get to know God, better."

As Josh said the words he felt something inside him dissolve. As they stood there in the office he was aware of tears on his cheeks, but he didn't mind. The peace and acceptance that washed over him made everything else seem of little importance.

"Well, first you need to say thank-you," Kyra told him, still holding on to him. "After that, we can work on other stuff, but for me at least, once you can say thank-you almost everything else gets easier by comparison."

Somehow they ended up in chairs in the family waiting room for more than an hour, Josh never letting go of Kyra's hand. Holding on to her as if she were a lifeline, Josh listened while she told him a story. It was *the* story, the only story that mattered, full of love and forgiveness, and by the end it sounded so simple Josh couldn't figure out why he hadn't really heard it like this years before.

But that didn't matter because he'd heard it now, and in his heart Josh knew that nothing in his life would ever be quite the same again.

EIGHT

In the week they waited for the DNA tests to be done, Kyra spent most of the time alternating between throwing herself into work and wanting to pace like a tiger in a cage. Finally Allie came into her office with papers in hand. "You have a match," she said simply, putting the results on Kyra's desk.

Kyra was sorry that Josh wasn't in the room to share the moment. He'd be back soon, though, and she could tell him that "Abigail" was actually Nikki. "Now we have a way to put you at rest," Kyra said, knowing that she was talking to someone who couldn't hear her anymore. She praised God that she had been able to be a part of this. Every time she was able to bring closure to someone, to help solve the mystery of a person's identity or a cause of death, she felt that she was doing what she was called to do.

When she told Josh that two hours later, he looked mystified. "Maybe I just haven't ever hung around church people enough, but I have no idea what you're talking about when you say 'called' like that. Is it like that 'road to Jerusalem' thing with bright lights and a voice?"

"Damascus," she said gently. "Saul was on the road to Damascus. And no, it's nothing that dramatic. It's just this welling up in me of something that says yes."

Josh looked at her, a wry grin on his face. "See, I don't even know the right territory, much less the right names. I thought it was Paul that got hit by that lightning bolt or whatever it was, anyway."

"Later he was Paul. That day he was still Saul. It's a pretty amazing story if you want to read it."

Josh shrugged. "I never get that far in the Bible. I always get hung up someplace near the front, where they have that part that's all rules and stuff."

"I think you mean Leviticus. And you're right, that's tough reading sometimes." Kyra had a thought, and she stood up from her desk and looked in the bookshelves over by the window of the office. "Here, this might help. Give this one a try and maybe it will make more sense to you. It's called *The Message,* and while it's not the world's deepest study Bible or anything, it's good to start out with."

Josh turned it over in his hands, and Kyra saw light make sparkles on the bright plastic cover. "And I notice this one is just the New Testament. Does that perhaps mean that it leaves out the rule book?"

"That particular one does. But this has some rules in it, too. Jesus says his rules are easy, though. You might even agree with that once you've read through this."

"We'll see. Will this explain that 'call' thing we were talking about before?"

"Once you get deep enough into it, yes. But not right away. I'd have to say that 'call' means that it feels like you're doing what you're supposed to do, what you were made to do."

His face looked wistful. "Wow. It's been a while since I felt that way. I got feelings like that sometimes in the bureau, especially when I thought I was chasing down something related to my dad. But since that all ended, I haven't gotten that feeling much."

"What about trying to find out these girls' identities? You seem to have really flung yourself into that."

Now he gave her a half smile, quirking up one corner of his mouth. "Yeah, I guess I did. Maybe this notion of 'call' makes a little more sense than I thought."

He sat quietly for a few minutes, turning the book over in his hands. "That's the first piece of the puzzle, anyway. Now we have to figure out who did this and why. And if he's still around…which I'm afraid he is…we need to bring him in."

"That's true. At least somebody needs to bring him in. But remember, Josh, that this office is concerned with forensics and evidence that will build a case against the murderer. The state police have homicide investigators who will take over when we're done. And I have to tell you that we're getting close to done."

Josh nodded. "I know that. But when I hand this over, I want to give those investigators every possible piece of information that I can."

"I can't argue with that. Just make sure that you stay objective. I'm not comfortable with the way you've focused on one particular suspect."

"Do you know something about anybody connected with this case that you haven't shared with me? Because so far I haven't found anything that tells me I shouldn't count Ramon Garcia as a prime suspect."

When Josh got stirred up, his eyes flashed with a glint that showed silver in the pale blue. The glint was there now, making Kyra remember that he'd spent a decade as an FBI agent. "So show me something that would back up your feelings. That, and talk to the other people involved to make sure that you don't find something that should make us suspect them."

He sat up straighter. "That's usually how I do my job. If you want to know more about the investigative part of your department, why don't you come with me?"

"I will, for some of it. It's time I knew more about that end of what we do. I haven't had the chance to check it out before because we've been clearing this case and a dozen others. But right now this is the most important thing we've got going and I want to see it from all angles."

"Great. I'll make sure that I can show you all the angles that I can."

Joshua stretched in front of his computer, trying to loosen all the cramped muscles and tight joints from too long a stay in this chair checking records. It was worth the effort. Ramon Garcia was deeper in his sights than ever, but neither of the other guys with connections to more than one of the young women could be ruled out, either.

Judging from what he'd found today, their next job should be to talk to Deon Quinn and ask a lot of questions. If Quinn really wanted to go into law enforcement, he had some explaining to do about his past. Josh didn't feel bad about asking any of the questions, because he knew the young man would have to answer even tougher ones to get admitted to a police academy.

Two days later Josh and Kyra sat in a coffee shop in Silver Springs with Deon Quinn. He'd agreed to meet them about a mile from the mall where he worked as a security guard. Still in his blue uniform, the young man stared down at a cooling coffee. "I know that what you found doesn't look good. But I had my wild times a long time ago. That record you found may not have been juvenile, but it's nearly ten years old. When my son was born, everything changed."

"And why was that? It doesn't appear that you spent all that much time with him." Kyra's voice sounded cold. It made Josh wonder what had happened in her life to make her appear hostile to this young man. Maybe it was as simple as the fact that he was only three years younger than she was and his life was so scattered. Or maybe it had something to do with what she might have perceived as a child's neglect.

"I've been in his life from the first even when I haven't lived with him. It's more than I can say about my own father. He was out of the picture before I turned four."

"So your mom raised you?" The question came from Kyra again.

Quinn shrugged. "My grandma, mostly. Mom was working two jobs a lot of the time just to keep us together. When I was a little kid I didn't understand that. I just knew that she was never there."

"And now she's raising your son." Josh tried to keep his voice level, nonjudgmental. It was hard.

"Not for long. And I see Andre at least twice a week. More when I can. I'm trying to build a future for him. For all of us."

"Don't get so busy building that future that you forget the present, Mr. Quinn." Kyra's tone was even sharper. "Kids need attention all the time. And the next few months may be hard on the whole family now that Gen's death has been brought up again."

"My mom's relieved," Deon said, his dark eyes clouded with pain. "She never thought Gen would just walk away from her son. Now we can tell Andre for sure that his mom cared for him and didn't want to leave him."

"What about you? How do you feel about all of this?" Josh decided to push the question, to see how Deon would react. So far Quinn had talked about everybody's feelings but his own. How he expressed his own feelings would tell them a lot about his capacity for violence.

"I guess I'm glad. When Gen disappeared it was rough, really rough. We were both eighteen, a time when life should have been opening up in front of us, but that wasn't the way things were happening. Neither of us had a decent job or a good education. The system was the only way she knew to get by and she had just aged out. I was still living with Mama…my grandmother…while my mother worked fifty or more hours a week."

"Where was Andre?" Josh had uncomfortable visions of a toddler alone in a strange place.

"He was with me and Mama. Gen and I traded off once in a while so she could look for a job or something like that. The last time I talked to her she was all excited about some guy she said was going to help her get into a career. Not a job, a career. That's the way she put it."

"Do you remember any more? At this point anything helps." Kyra leaned forward, green eyes wide and attentive.

"That's about it. I think the guy's name was Ray, and I know it all had something to do with being a medical assistant. Gen said this guy told her it was the wave of the future and it only needed a three-month training class before she could start making real money."

"And real money was important for a couple of kids who hadn't finished high school."

Quinn straightened up and glared at Josh. "We both got our GED. But yeah, I won't argue that money was important. It still is if I'm going to make a real home for my son." He put his hands flat on the table, pushed his chair away and stood up. "Are we done here? Because I need to get back to work."

"We're done, for now. But we'll be staying in

touch." If Quinn was going to play the tough guy, he would, too. Kyra looked from one to the other without saying much. Josh could tell that she would have ended the interview differently. Maybe next time he'd let her call the shots.

They let Deon leave the coffee shop first and Josh watched him get into his small car. "Is this the way your part of the job usually works? Because it felt kind of abrupt to me. There were a couple of questions I would still like to ask him."

"Me, too. But we might as well let him feel like he has some control of the situation for now. We learned a lot here, and one thing I heard makes me want to go straight back to that medical clinic."

Kyra tilted her head, looking confused. "Were we listening to the same conversation? What did you hear that I didn't?"

"The part about Gen's great new career in medicine, courtesy of a guy named Ray."

She was silent for a moment, and then perked up. "Ah. Does this mean you think Gen's Ray might be Ramon Garcia?"

"It's a possibility, and one I want to explore. I needed one more reason to check out Garcia on a deeper level, anyway. And then there's Griffith."

"Gary Griffith? Do you think we should investigate him?"

"Oh, yeah. We've turned up three guys that have connections with at least two of the women and he's one of them. We may both think somebody else is the

GET 2 FREE BOOKS!

HURRY!
Return this card today to get **2 FREE Books** *and* **2 FREE** *Bonus Gifts!*

Love Inspired.
SUSPENSE

YES! *Please send me the 2 FREE Love Inspired® Suspense books and 2 FREE gifts for which I qualify. I understand that I am under no obligation to purchase anything further, as explained on the back of this card.*

affix
free
books
sticker
here

323 IDL ERRT

123 IDL ERQ5

FIRST NAME

LAST NAME

ADDRESS

APT.#

CITY

STATE/PROV.

ZIP/POSTAL CODE

Steeple
Hill®

▼ DETACH AND MAIL CARD TODAY! ▼

® and ™ are trademarks owned and used by the trademark owner and/or its licensee.
© 2007 STEEPLE HILL BOOKS

LISUS-LA-08

Steeple Hill Reader Service—Here's How It Works:

Accepting your 2 free books and 2 free gifts places you under no obligation to buy anything. You may keep the books and gifts and return the shipping statement marked "cancel." If you do not cancel, about a month later we will send you 4 additional books and bill you just $4.24 each in the U.S. or $4.74 each in Canada, plus 25¢ shipping & handling per book and applicable taxes if any.* That's the complete price, and — compared to cover prices of $5.50 each in the U.S. and $6.50 each in Canada — it's quite a bargain! You may cancel at any time, but if you choose to continue, every month we'll send you 4 more books, which you may either purchase at the discount price...or return to us and cancel your subscription.

*Terms and prices subject to change without notice. Sales tax applicable in N.Y. Canadian residents will be charged applicable provincial taxes and GST. All orders subject to approval. Books received may not be as shown. Credit or debit balances in a customer's account(s) may be offset by any other outstanding balance owed by or to the customer. Please allow 4 to 6 weeks for delivery. Offer available while quantities last.

If offer card is missing write to: Steeple Hill Reader Service, 3010 Walden Ave., P.O. Box 1867, Buffalo, NY 14240-1867

BUSINESS REPLY MAIL
FIRST-CLASS MAIL   PERMIT NO. 717   BUFFALO, NY

POSTAGE WILL BE PAID BY ADDRESSEE

STEEPLE HILL READER SERVICE
3010 WALDEN AVE
PO BOX 1867
BUFFALO NY 14240-9952

NO POSTAGE
NECESSARY
IF MAILED
IN THE
UNITED STATES

most likely possibility, but I'm not going to let Griffith go without at least talking to him."

Kyra shrugged. "Suit yourself. It's difficult for me to imagine that Diana would stay married to someone capable of crimes like this, or have a child with anybody she didn't trust."

"Does this mean you want to come with me when I talk to them? If you can keep from making up your mind beforehand and stay fairly quiet, you're welcome."

Kyra wrinkled her nose. "Well, thanks for thinking so highly of me." And before he could defend his remarks, she breezed out of the coffee shop, leaving him to follow.

He still felt like he was trying to catch up to her the next day. She'd found ways to mostly avoid him all morning. It wasn't as uncomfortable as it had been after he'd told her she'd had an easy life, but she wasn't real cordial, either.

Finally about one she came into their shared office again and he got up from the computer right away. "We need to talk. I don't want some kind of wall between us again. It's too hard to share an office and work on the same case with friction between us. Besides, it's no fun."

Until that last sentence Kyra had looked serious. With the last bit, she gave him the ghost of a smile. "You're right about that. And there's precious little fun in this job a lot of the time. But we've got to agree on a few things. For one, you can't keep making assumptions about me."

Ouch. She was right there. "It's hard not to. I spend most of my time making assumptions about people and sometimes it slips over into my personal life."

Kyra gave a short laugh. "Are you sure that came out right? I'm not sure we should describe anything going on between the two of us as our personal life. Won't that just make it harder to share work space, or work?"

"I think it's already too late to worry about that." Josh hadn't thought about it before he answered her, but now he realized that it was true. "What we've got is personal, and it's work. And it's different from anything else I've ever been a part of. How about you?"

She didn't take long to answer. "The same. I haven't had a lot of relationships with men, but this definitely feels like something out of the ordinary. That probably means we both need to be careful."

Josh nodded, feeling his mouth go dry. "Do you still want to go with me to talk to the Griffiths?"

Kyra's green eyes widened. "I don't think so. Maybe we need some time apart. Do you want me to call Diana and set things up? I can do that much."

"Sure. You already have the contact with her. That will make things easier. Thanks, Kyra."

"You're welcome. Just don't make me regret doing this."

He felt an incredible surge of protectiveness for her and his mouth was even drier. "You can count on me."

He thought he saw a flicker of pain in her eyes, and then it was gone. "I hope you're right. Normally I don't count on anybody but God. Life is just easier that way."

Josh shook his head. "To me that sounds a lot harder than counting on another human being. And for me, that's one of the most difficult things I can think of."

"See, that's something we can agree on, even though it's for different reasons. We both find it hard to trust other people." Kyra turned back toward her desk. "I think you'll understand very quickly, though, why I find Diana Griffith easier to trust than most people."

Sitting in the Griffiths' living room, Josh saw what Kyra meant. Diana Griffith could only be described as sweet-looking and warm. Her light brown hair framed her face in short curls that made her look only slightly older than the six teens living in the group home that she and her husband, Gary, ran. "I'm so sorry to hear that it was Nikki that you found. I always hoped that she was out there somewhere, that maybe she had made it to Alaska."

"Alaska?" Joshua had found that just echoing someone's statement sometimes led to a lot more information.

Diana nodded. "Most of the girls that live with us come from pretty rough family situations if there's any family at all. The ones that aren't too beaten down have a focus or a dream. For Nikki that was Alaska. She always said that someday she was going to live there, with the moose and the elk and the polar bears."

Josh knew his expression gave him away when Diana laughed softly. "Okay, you and I know as adults that there are no polar bears in most of Alaska, but I wasn't about to tell an eleven-year-old that. I had to give her enough bad news without that kind."

"How long did she stay with you?"

Diana looked up toward the ceiling, with an expression that said she was counting in her head. "Almost three years. It was the longest she ever stayed anywhere. If she hadn't started acting out, she would have been here even longer. Who knows, maybe if that had happened…"

"It's no good second-guessing yourself, Mrs. Griffith. It sounds as if you provided as good an environment as possible for Nikki. You said she acted out. What happened?"

"She was fighting with the other girls here, the younger ones, and things got way too physical. We couldn't take the added stress in the house just then. I was pregnant with Sarah and we couldn't get Nikki turned around. Then she ran away and that tipped the scale. Four months later I heard that she had been found and put into a…structured facility."

"Does that mean juvenile detention?" Josh didn't like euphemisms if there was a way around them.

Diana looked away from him for a moment, pushing her lips into a tense line. "Not exactly. This would have been somewhere between the kind of home we have here and detention." Before she could say more a sound outside made Diana rise from the armchair where she sat. "I heard car doors. You'll have to give me a minute."

Josh watched as she went to the front door and

opened it. Two girls came in, letting a blast of damp spring air in with them. "It's raining!" the younger one exclaimed. "We got all wet."

She had a delighted giggle and springy curls accentuated by the humidity. Josh had to guess that she was about seven. "Mr. Richards, this is my daughter, Sarah, and Jackie. Besides Sarah she's the youngest of our kids right now and she goes to the same school as Sarah." While she spoke Diana gave each girl a hug. "Now, both of you go upstairs and change out of your school clothes and take off those wet shoes, okay?"

In a flurry of backpacks and jackets the children did as they were told. Diana nodded toward the back of the house. "We're going to have to move this conversation to the kitchen while I get snacks ready. If those two are home, it means that Gary should be home with the middle-schoolers in about ten minutes. He picks them up on his way home from work at the hospital and they get here right after the grade-school carpool."

With an ease that told Josh that it was her normal routine, the woman pulled a box of graham crackers out of the pantry and lined up five mugs on the kitchen countertop, spooning cocoa mix into them. Josh watched her with a twinge he recognized as guilt at his momentary envy for the kids in her care. Nobody had ever met him after school with cookies and hot chocolate.

He was still castigating himself for the thought when the back door opened a few minutes later and two more slightly older girls came in, followed by a man closing an umbrella. "It's pouring out there.

Weatherman was wrong again," he grumbled. Josh looked at him as he took off a light jacket and hung it on a coatrack, laying the wet umbrella under the rack. "Gary Griffith," he said, sticking out his hand to Josh, who introduced himself.

"Diana told me you were coming. Do you want to go back to the living room and talk, away from the commotion in here?"

Josh followed his lead back to the living room as Griffith eased through a swinging door between the two rooms. "She also told me about Nikki," he said softly to Josh. "I don't want any of those kids unduly upset. They have enough to worry them without something like this." The concern in his dark eyes looked real, and after only a few more minutes talking to Griffith Josh was ready to go. He needed to go back to the office for a discussion with Kyra. It was time to try to convince her that they needed to issue a warrant before Ramon Garcia got away from them.

NINE

Kyra looked up from her paperwork when Josh came into the office. He didn't look happy, but he didn't seem terribly upset, either. "Okay, prepare to be surprised," he told her, pulling a chair up to her desk. "I totally agree with you on something."

"Oh? That is a surprise." Kyra couldn't remember too many times in their work on this case when the two of them had been in agreement on anything. "Does this have to do with Diana and Gary Griffith?"

"It does. And after talking to her for a while, and seeing her with the kids there, it's hard for me to imagine that she could have anything to do with one murder, let alone three."

While Josh talked, Kyra watched him. His hair had gotten noticeably longer in the time they'd been working together. She realized that it was a good indication of how much time they'd been spending on work. Every night when she went home, Ranger wound around her ankles with an ongoing feline commentary on how he felt about her long hours in the lab.

Obviously Josh had spent so much time on the case and driving back and forth to his apartment in Virginia that he didn't have time for a haircut.

She must have been thinking about all of this longer than she realized because Josh was looking at her, blue eyes sparkling. "You still with me?"

"Yes. I'm sorry about that. I was truly paying attention, but then I started looking at your hair."

His brows drew down and together. "What's wrong with my hair? I know I've combed it at least once today. It was raining when I left the group home, but I didn't think it did that much damage."

"No, it's not that," she tried to reassure him. "It's just that it's gotten so much longer while we've been working together. You haven't even had time for a haircut."

Josh ran a hand through the gingery mass, starting to get slightly wavy. "You're right. I kind of like it this length, though. I'd been keeping it shorter than normal while I'd done some undercover work. Unless you think I should cut it, this is good."

"That length is fine," she said, pushing away the wish to run her fingers through his hair as well. She could imagine the texture, thick and smooth under her fingertips. "So we agree on Diana. Tell me what you thought of Gary."

Josh shrugged. "He doesn't immediately make me cautious like Garcia does. He brings the kids home from school, worries about talking about death in front of them and seems to have a clean record at work."

"So you haven't been just checking out Ramon Garcia?"

Josh smiled briefly. "Even though I still suspect him, it would be foolish not to check out anybody that could have as much possibility as Griffith or Deon Quinn."

"My kind of investigation usually takes place mostly within the lab," she told him. "I'm not used to being a part of this kind of search involving live people."

"That's why they wanted me here. And I have to admit that I've enjoyed it a lot more than I thought I would. When I started I wasn't looking forward to my time here. It felt like a punishment or a demotion."

Kyra wrinkled her nose. "Even working with me? Thanks for the compliment."

"Hey, that's not the way I meant it. I was just unhappy about being out of the bureau and way out here in the boonies. Working with you was probably the one positive this assignment had going for it."

She found herself smiling as she listened to Josh backpedal, and watching him earnestly try to get out of the hole he'd dug for himself with his words. It was on the tip of her tongue to tell him how fluttery she'd felt when he started working at the crime lab. But she kept that to herself and let him stew just a little while longer. "Okay, let's drop this train of thought and go back to talking about the investigation. Why did you look at Quinn and Griffith if you're so sure that Garcia is your prime suspect?"

"Exactly because Garcia *is* the prime suspect. If I have to testify in court I want to be able to say that we checked out everybody who had the same kinds of means, motive or opportunity that he had. And all that is why I think it's time to get a warrant to look at Garcia even closer."

He looked so eager that Kyra hated disappointing him. "Josh, this is where it's going to get hard for you. Our job is wrapping up here. Now that we know who the victims are and have a rough idea of how long they've been dead, we become the support team for Homicide."

His face fell. "You mean that you don't follow up any of the rest of the investigation? Before when you've worked with me on FBI cases I always kept you in the loop on how things turned out."

Kyra nodded. "Was that policy for the bureau, or professional courtesy?"

Josh looked down at the floor. "I guess it wasn't policy."

Kyra pushed on, hoping she could do things without being too blunt. "And you were in charge there, Josh. Here, the state of Maryland is running the show and you're just an investigator on loan because you have experience. Technically there's not a solid reason for the FBI to get involved."

"Which means I have no official standing here. That's a new experience for me and I don't like it," Josh admitted. "How do you handle just letting things go like this?"

"It's what I do. I am responsible for identifying the victims, creating a timeline, and when I can, telling the state police how someone died. Past that, I'm out of my area of expertise."

"Yeah, well, I consider this my area of expertise all right, and I want you to figure out how I get transferred on to the homicide team that's going to take over. At the least I need to brief them on everything we've got so far and talk to somebody who wants to chase down Garcia pretty quickly."

"I'm pretty sure that a transfer isn't going to work. Didn't you tell me that you were specifically assigned to my office for the duration of this case?" Kyra saw him wince a little at the accuracy of her assessment of the situation.

"So what about being a consultant? Or a liaison from this office? You just said this isn't your area of expertise. Maybe you need somebody to follow up on investigations like this one that are bound to be high profile."

Kyra sighed. "I'm glad I'm on the same side of the law that you are, Joshua. You're extremely determined."

"I pride myself on it." His eyes were blue steel. "That isn't much of an answer." He stepped close to her, and Kyra stopped breathing for a moment while she drank in his power and intensity. If it had been hard earlier to resist touching him, running a hand through his hair, it was twice as difficult now. The spicy scent of his cologne and the warmth of his breath, which she could feel at this distance, didn't make things any easier.

"I could probably answer you better if you weren't so close to me," Kyra admitted. It was difficult to form coherent thoughts standing this near to Josh.

"Me, too, but now that I'm this close, for some reason I don't want to move." His voice was softer, husky. They touched each other at the same instant; Kyra could feel his hands in the middle of her back while she felt his ribs expand with his breath.

The room was silent for what seemed like a very long time, but was really only seconds before he bent his head slightly and kissed her. His lips were warm for a moment. Before they could feel warmer he pulled away, letting go of her and stepping back a pace. "I'd apologize, except I think that was mutual."

Kyra nodded, not trusting herself to speak quite yet. "If that was an effort to convince me we shouldn't be in the same office all day, it won't work. I agreed to have you as an investigator for this department and it has to stay that way. But I'll make sure that you get as much connection with the serious crimes unit as possible, okay?"

He shrugged slightly. "It's going to have to do. When I came over here, Pam Gorman gave me the choice of taking this assignment or going on full paid leave for at least six weeks, so I expect she wants me out of the office at least that long. Since I imagine she's not ready to have me back this soon, I'm pretty much at your mercy."

Josh looked at her with intensity, then sighed softly. "With some people that would be a bad thing, but I think I can handle it as long as it's you."

As he left the room, Kyra found herself shivering slightly, tiny tremors of excitement up her spine. Their brief kiss had been wonderful. Now, how did she keep from having it happen again?

It was Saturday afternoon, and this time Josh wasn't even asking himself how he got involved with another one of Kyra's activities. The truth was that he enjoyed being with her most of the time and he'd agreed to join her on this outing almost before he knew what it was.

So here they were, he and Kyra, Jasmine and Ashley in his car heading to a church, but not to worship. "Are we going to do potatoes again?" Jasmine asked from the backseat, a light whine in her voice. "Because if we are, somebody else is going to have to dump out the bag into the sink. I never saw potatoes that big and gnarly before in my life."

"My foster mom has a dog that's smaller than those potatoes," Ashley chimed in.

"Okay, enough already. We're going the same place we were before and the menu hasn't changed, so I expect there will be potatoes. We can probably talk Mr. Richards into dumping the potatoes, and maybe even scrubbing them. That way you two can chop a couple of pounds of veggies or crack three or four dozen eggs."

There was a sigh in stereo from the backseat. Josh kept his eyes on the road and kept from laughing. Now he looked forward to seeing these potatoes.

The church was a large complex on the outskirts of Baltimore, so big that it had a restaurant-size kitchen attached. There were people bustling around it in twos and threes, all set to different tasks. A smiling man who looked like everybody's grandpa and introduced himself as Jim greeted them and drew them around a large steel worktable.

"Tomorrow at seven in the morning another crew of people this size or larger will load a truck with ten pans of breakfast casseroles, enough doughnuts to fill a car trunk, ten gallons of fruit salad and enough orange juice for three football teams. They'll be taking all of that to a park three miles from here, where we'll serve somewhere between one-hundred-fifty and two-hundred people breakfast. Another crew will provide a worship service. What you're doing this afternoon will make that breakfast possible."

He went on to give them instructions on what to do at their stations and asked if they had any questions. Ashley raised her hand, and Jim smiled and said, "This isn't school, young lady. Go ahead and ask your question."

She looked down at the floor for a moment, tracing a circle with the toe of her tennis shoe. "I forgot to ask last time. How come you do that so early? At seven it's just barely light and it's still pretty cold out."

"Yes, but that's when the homeless shelters start telling people they have to leave," Jim said softly. "That means most of our worshipers will be hungry and looking for a place to be."

Ashley nodded as if she understood, and Jim pointed her and Josh to a sink where the dreaded bag of potatoes sat on the drain board. Josh got the bag open and dumped them into the large sink, impressed by the thumps they made when they landed.

He gave a low whistle. "Wow. I thought you two were kidding about the potatoes. What does your foster mom have, a Yorkie or a Chihuahua?"

"Chihuahua," Ashley said, using two hands to pick up the biggest, knottiest tuber in the sink. "And he's way smaller than this thing. But Mr. Jim says that because they're so weird-looking, Food Share gives them potatoes like this for free, so they can feed more people that way."

"That's cool." Josh hefted one himself and turned on the water in the sink. "At least there won't be too many of them to scrub in a fifty-pound bag."

"Yeah, but wait till you start peeling them. It's like trying to peel a football," Ashley said, grabbing a scrub brush to work on her portion of the bag.

Behind them at a worktable, Josh saw Kyra and Jasmine stemming grapes and putting them in a large colander. Ashley followed his gaze and Jasmine looked up at the other girl. "I could have told you why they get to the park so early, Ash. The shelters don't cut anybody any slack. Some of them start moving people out of there by six-thirty. No time to get a shower or brush your teeth or anything."

Josh watched the two of them, feeling a lump in his throat at the thought that this slender teen knew about homeless shelters from the inside. Where was God in something like that? he thought.

Kyra must have seen some of what he was feeling because she came over and put a hand on his arm gently. "We'll talk once we get the girls home, okay?"

"Sure," he said. By then he'd probably have half-a-dozen questions just as unanswerable as this one. But before that, he needed to go back to scrubbing potatoes. He soon discovered that Ashley was right about peeling them. Whether he tried a paring knife or a peeler, it wasn't easy. And the women who were operating a large food processor at another station in the kitchen groaned when they saw the bowl he carried to them.

The older of the two handed him a cutting board and a knife the size of a meat cleaver. "Here. See if you can chop those monster spuds into chunks the size of a regular potato. That way we can chop them enough to cook them in one of those skillets at the stove."

He nodded and went back to work. This was the first time he'd ever tried to prepare food or cook in these kinds of proportions. It surprised him to discover just how much hard work went into making breakfast for a crowd.

Two hours later Kyra came to find him as he cleaned off a worktable, polishing the stainless steel back to a shine. "You look like you're about as ready as we are to leave," she said with a smile. "I promised the girls a stop at a coffeehouse before we took them back."

"Yeah, as long as Jasmine just gets a decaf latte," Ashley piped up.

"I hope you ladies don't mind if I get the real thing. Unless I boost my energy with something, I may have to crawl up the stairs to my apartment." All of them laughed at that, and Josh didn't tell them he was only half joking.

The large cappuccino that he got helped give him a second wind, along with the brownies he brought back to the table with the coffee. "I know they're big," he said, trying to forestall any complaints from Kyra, "so I just got two for all four of us. I hope that's okay."

Kyra sighed. "I guess so. Even half of one of those will give me back more calories than I burned all afternoon. But they do look good."

The girls agreed with her, and Josh had a challenge keeping half of one of the brownies for himself. Jasmine distracted him twice before he realized that she was breaking off corners from his piece every time she drew his attention elsewhere.

He didn't call her on it because he figured that she probably had enough problems in life right now. Besides, he'd always heard that pregnant women were extremely emotional; he could only imagine what carrying a child did to a teenager's already-unstable emotions.

Instead he moved his plate quietly closer to Ashley and kept listening to the questions she was asking Kyra.

"How come God lets people be homeless?" she prodded while Kyra sat quietly. "You keep saying God can do anything, so why doesn't God fix it so everybody has a place to live?"

"Maybe He's trying to get us to do what we're supposed to," Jasmine said. "Or maybe He just doesn't care."

Kyra looked straight at the girl and shook her head. "Nope. I can't believe that God doesn't care about us. I think God cares about us like nobody else does, or even can. God loves us so much that Jesus came to die for us. For each of us. That doesn't sound like a God who doesn't care to me."

Jasmine gave a halfhearted shrug. "I guess you're right. It's just that sometimes it's hard to convince myself that anybody cares, even God."

Josh wondered how much to say at this point. Kyra seemed to be doing a pretty good job of helping Jasmine, but what she said really stirred something in him. He took a breath and gathered his courage. "I've felt that way, too, Jasmine." Across the table he could see Kyra's eyes widen. She probably would never have expected him to speak up. "But since I've gotten to know Kyra better, she's shown me what she believes about God, and it's harder for me to believe that God doesn't care. Even though I don't feel it all the time, I think that Kyra's right and God doesn't ever leave us totally alone."

Out of the corner of his eye, he could see Kyra make a conscious effort to close her gaping mouth. He was glad, because her jaw had been so low that for a moment she reminded him of a fish out of water.

Jasmine's lower lip trembled for a moment. "That's easy for you to say." She pulled her slender body upright in the chair. "You are an adult with your own place to live, a job and a car. You can do what you want most of the time and nobody can make you do what they want instead."

Josh fought laughter because he knew it wouldn't help the situation. "It's true that I have an apartment and a job, and a car to drive, but the rest of that stuff you said isn't exactly right. It's because I have a job that plenty of people can tell me what to do. Sometimes those are things I'd choose to do on my own, but a lot of the time that's not the case. And there's a downside to all this adult stuff. When I go home at night to that apartment, there's nobody else there."

Jasmine looked thoughtful. "I'd like that for a couple of hours. Then I'd probably get bored or lonely and I'd want to have other people around. Why don't you at least get yourself a dog?"

"Not home enough to take care of one," Josh told her. "And I'm a little bit allergic. I'm finding out that I like animals more than I thought. Right now if I want to have one around, I'd follow Miss Kyra home and wrestle with her cat."

Kyra looked like she almost spit out a mouthful of coffee. "*Wrestle with my cat?* Why would you even think of doing that?"

"Because he's the size of a puma," Josh countered, happy to see that the girls were grinning. "Have you ever looked at the paws on that beast? He can probably catch two different mice at once, or maybe even a rat. I'd pity the rat that ran into him."

Kyra shook her head. "You'll give these two nightmares, Joshua. They don't know you're teasing about my sweet kitty."

Ashley looked disappointed. "Are you? If so that's too bad. I was just thinking that maybe we could borrow him for a little while. I'd feel a lot safer with a puma around." Ashley's voice was so soft Josh wasn't sure he'd really heard her say what he thought.

He was right back to square one here, ready to protect these kids whether they wanted his protection or not. It was all he could do not to pound the table with his clenched fist. Over the girls' heads Kyra seemed to be sending him a silent message of thanks for keeping things as calm as possible.

"So what's up that you would want a puma, Ashley? Is somebody bothering you at school?" It was the first problem that Josh could think of that a young teen might have.

She shook her head, looking down at the table. "No, nothing like that. The other girls in my house laugh at me because they think I'm imagining things. But something feels…I don't know…creepy." Her cheeks were red now and Josh could tell she wasn't going to say anything else.

"Have you been watching anything scary on TV? Or reading any of those vampire books we talked about before?" Kyra's hand rested on the girl's arm and her voice was gentle.

"A little TV, but none of those books. You convinced me I didn't want to do that," Ashley said.

Jasmine had been taking this all in with narrowed eyes and a slight scowl. "Maybe those girls in your house are right. Maybe you're just scaring yourself with made-up stuff."

Ashley looked on the verge of tears and Josh felt at such a loss. Female tears were one of those things he'd never been able to handle. "No matter what's scaring Ashley, if it feels real to her it's still going to scare her. Is there anything we can do to help?" At this point Josh would have taken on a real puma just to make this slight kid feel better.

She was silent for quite some time. "Maybe we could pray about it. That's what you say you do, isn't it, Kyra?"

"It sure is. Do you want to pray here or in the car?"

"In the car," Ashley said, to Josh's relief. For these kids he would have tried praying even here in the middle of a crowded place, but the relative quiet of the car sounded better. He still wished that Ashley's problem could have been solved with a puma or some firearms. Those were the kinds of weapons he felt more comfortable with. Would he ever come to a point where relying on prayer felt better than relying on the automatic in his holster? For now, he knew, cold steel was more of a comfort.

TEN

"So, are you going home now or do you want to come in to wrestle the cat?" Kyra teased as she got ready to get out of Josh's car in her driveway.

"If you're really offering, I'd like to come in." His expression was a lot more serious than she expected. "I want to talk a little bit more about what Ashley said."

"Sure. I can put a pot of tea on if you like, and maybe even light a fire in the fireplace." The evening was turning cool and damp, and Kyra felt chilled. A cup of tea and watching flickering flames sounded pretty good after the workout of the afternoon.

"I won't stay long," Josh said. "You have to be tired and we've got another long week ahead of us at work. Or at least I expect we do."

"Yes, we will. You'll be around that much longer to help tie things up, if you're wondering." She would be if she were the temporary employee. "Although I have to imagine you're about ready to get back to the FBI and some real investigative work."

She unlocked the door and Josh followed her in.

"Ranger. Hey, furry guy," she called out, listening for the thump that would indicate the cat's heavy body scooting to the floor after a nap someplace he wasn't supposed to be. He strolled out from the kitchen, making *rowr*-ing feline conversation. "Yeah, we caught you, didn't we? You know you're not supposed to be anywhere near that countertop, even the stools."

If Ranger felt guilty, he didn't show it. He came into the front room with ears perked up and tail high, then wound sinuously around Josh's ankles. "I think he actually remembers me." He reached down and scratched behind the cat's ears. "Sure, you're a puma, aren't you?"

"I don't believe you two." Kyra had to laugh. She hadn't seen her cat warm up to anybody like this. Usually he was a bit standoffish; definitely choosy about who he made up with. Here he was following Josh around, hardly letting him settle into one of the kitchen chairs before he jumped up in his lap.

"You don't have to put up with that," she told Josh. "I know you're allergic to him."

"I'll try to forget that for a few minutes. He's a nice guy and I'm enjoying the attention. When I was talking to the girls about the joys of adult life, I meant most of what I said. The worst part is going back to that empty apartment."

"Especially when it's that far a drive," Kyra said as she put loose tea in the teapot and turned the burner on under the kettle. "How long does it take you to get to work or home these days?"

"Longer than it does to get to the bureau, but I brought that on myself. Funny thing is I'm not ready to go back there yet." Josh looked puzzled, rubbing Ranger's head thoughtfully. The cat gave a rumbling purr and settled down in his lap.

"That's been a change since you first got to my lab." Kyra crossed over to the fireplace and set the kindling under the already-laid fire and lit it. She usually kept things ready this way, so that she could come home from a long day and have a fire quickly.

"I guess that was pretty obvious, huh? I felt like I was being banished out here to the boonies because my supervisor didn't want to deal with me. Thinking it over, now I can see that I was a disaster waiting to happen."

"Whoa. That's a pretty strong statement."

Josh nodded. "I was taking some pretty strong...and very stupid...actions. For years I'd had a purpose, a goal. I wanted to prove that my father didn't really commit suicide, or do the other things he'd been accused of. Once I'd done that I wasn't sure what to do with myself. I just didn't care much anymore."

"And that's changed?" Kyra found herself almost holding her breath, waiting for his answer. "What made things different?"

"You," Josh said softly. "Seeing your passion for your job, the way you cared about people you didn't know, just because they were people."

Kyra felt tears prickle behind her eyelids. "Okay, now you're going to make me cry if you keep up like that," she told him. "And I've seen how that makes you react. So if tears make you uncomfortable, don't go there." Ranger had jumped off Josh's lap and come over to her, head-butting against her jeans in an effort to get some attention, or more likely food.

She filled the cat's dish and gave silent thanks when the teakettle began whistling. She needed to busy herself with something so Josh wouldn't see her reaction to what he'd said. Pouring the boiling water over the tea, she put the lid back on the pot and got out a couple of mugs.

"You saw how I reacted to Ashley, didn't you? That's what I actually came in here to talk about, anyway. Of the three girls I've met that are in the care system right now, she strikes me as the calmest. But she's the one who's nervous about something."

Kyra pondered how to answer him without disparaging Ashley or giving away any of her secrets. "She is probably the calmest on the surface, you're right. But she has a vivid imagination and she's very bright. Sometimes that's a great thing, but other times…"

"I heard you ask her about books and movies. Is she that suggestible?"

Kyra shrugged, still working out the answer for herself. "She got into these awful vampire stories a while back, and she couldn't even sleep without a light on for a month or so. You can imagine how the other kids teased her."

Josh winced, and Kyra wondered what memory she'd stirred up for him. "Yeah, I can. Wouldn't that make her less likely to say anything now?"

Kyra mulled that over while she poured tea and brought the mugs to the table. "Maybe it would. I hadn't looked at it that way." She sat down next to Josh, reaching for the sugar bowl and stirring a small spoonful into her tea. "You know, when we put our heads together we make a decent team."

She offered the sugar to Josh, who held out his hand to refuse. "I was thinking that, too. It surprises me because I haven't worked this well with a partner in years." He took a sip of tea and set the mug back down. "Except you, now that I think of it. Things have always gone smoother on investigations where I brought you in for some odd forensic puzzle."

His words warmed her face as much as the steam from her mug of tea. Kyra tried to look anywhere but at Josh's face. She was afraid that if she did he'd see what she felt, how much his words meant to her. "Maybe so. I know I enjoyed working with you. It probably influenced my decision to come over to crime work full-time as much as anything else."

"So without me you would have stayed in the academic world, lecturing and writing obscure papers on the life cycle of some kind of insects?"

Josh was one of the few people she'd ever known who could bring her from one end of the emotional spectrum to the other so quickly. She laughed. "You make it sound so awful."

"That's because to me it would be. Even in the lab you've probably noticed that I have to get up and walk around every half hour or so. I have to be on the move."

He took another sip of tea and looked down into the mug. "This is good. I didn't even ask what kind you were making, in case it was something full of twigs and leaves or something."

She stifled another giggle. "It is, kind of. Blackberry sage, not much caffeine and a flavor I thought would go nicely with wood smoke."

"And you were right. But I've probably taken up enough of your time. I've gotten at least one concern answered, and the cat is back to ignoring me now that he's been fed, so I ought to start that drive home."

He rose from the table and she stood with him. "It's still early," she said, not sure why she was arguing. She wanted to take a hot bath and slip into ratty flannel pj pants and an ancient T-shirt, something she wouldn't dream of doing with anybody else around.

"It is, but we've been together a long time today, Kyra, and I know we're going to be together a lot all week at work."

"So you're tired of me?" She tried to keep her tone light and not show any hurt.

"Just the opposite. If I'm going to keep things on a professional level for the rest of the week, I think it's time to go home." The intensity of his gaze almost made her lose her balance for a moment. She felt like pressing a palm to her chest like the shocked heroine in a cheesy movie.

"Okay, then. Maybe you're right." Now it was difficult for her to look at him without stirring feelings she'd rather keep dormant.

"I know I'm right, at least from my perspective. It's heartening to me that you might agree with me. Can I leave you with one thought to pull yourself back to business? I'm concerned that if Garcia is our killer, he's getting ready to get active again. That's why I'm inclined to take what Ashley said seriously."

Kyra swallowed hard, her heart beating faster now for an entirely different reason. "And Ashley, Marta and Jasmine are uncomfortably close to his earlier victim profile."

"Exactly. Tomorrow let's talk about what we can do to see that nothing happens to them." She followed him to the front door, where Josh paused for a moment.

"After that I can hardly say I hope you sleep well. Still, maybe you can get some rest and come in tomorrow with new ideas."

Kyra nodded and watched him head for his car. Now she was the one concerned, wondering if she would spend the night with visions of one of "her" girls as the victim of a killer.

And if your right eye offends you, pluck it out. That was the way the Bible verse went, wasn't it? The Watcher stood silently in one of the few places he could relax and tried not to think about the little girls. What if it wasn't your own eye that offended you, but somebody else's, like those girls were doing to him all the time now? They wouldn't stop staring at him, following him and asking for it. They were already evil. That was why they were where they were. He'd just be thinning the herd.

It would be harder now to carry it off, he knew. He was older and more experienced, but that wasn't going to work totally in his favor. He could probably escape detection easier, but the girls would be more suspicious of him than before. Still, he had some advantages. With what he did all day he was almost invisible to them. They never noticed him as a real person; they just looked at him with contempt the way they would some kind of bug on a windshield.

Where would he take them this time? His garden was out of the question. The yellow caution tape was still there, one side of the rectangle drooping a little but not enough to risk a visit. There was still the Other Place, but that might be dangerous. He'd taken *her* there and she might remember being there. True, it was a pretty ordinary place, but there was only one person who knew what it meant to him and was still alive.

Did she even remember? Perhaps he could gamble on her having too much to think about when they were there for the scene to really register. Maybe he should go back home and get on the computer and see if anything else had made it into the newspaper.

What had already been in there was bad enough. That bone doctor and her investigator hadn't just destroyed his garden. They'd made it impossible for him to even go back there and reminisce without fear of being caught. And now they'd identified the girls.

He imagined taking that doctor someplace and slowly tightening his hands around her slender neck. His fingers tingled with anticipation of doing it. She didn't look all that much bigger than Serita, anyway. He thought that was the name of the one who had put up the most struggle. She'd hurt him, but in the end it had worked out okay.

The rain began to fall harder, making the Watcher shiver a little. It was time to go home and figure out what to do. All he knew was that it was time to do something. Between the little girls daring him and his own inner voices urging them on, he had to do it soon.

"So, did you sleep any?" Kyra greeted Josh as he walked into the office balancing two large cups of coffee.

"Not a lot," he admitted. "But then I hadn't expected to." No sense telling her that it wasn't worry about their killer that had kept him up, but the look on her face last night when he'd told her how much trouble he was having keeping things professional between them.

He'd expected her to laugh, maybe, or be offended. Instead her deep green eyes had widened and she'd worn just the hint of a smile, a look that showed a bit of surprise and even more understanding and agreement. He'd kept replaying that look last night, wondering if he was reading a lot more into it than he should. It's not like she was declaring undying love for him or anything. She just seemed to agree that it might be getting hard to keep a professional distance between them.

So now he set the two cups down on his desk and turned on his laptop. While it came to life, he handed her one of the coffees. "Plain black, dark roast, no foo-foo. I got myself a latte and virtuously passed on the pastries for both of us."

"And I thank you for that. Can I pay you back for the coffee?"

"Nope. You'll buy sometime this week, I'm sure. Besides, yours was a lot cheaper than mine, anyway."

"Okay." She didn't waste any time on argument, going straight to the issues at hand. "I thought a lot about what you said last night. I'm not as convinced as you are that Garcia is the guy, but I'll agree that nobody else we've identified looks any better. And the thought that any of these kids that I know could be in danger makes my blood run cold."

She was pale just saying the words. Josh felt like patting her shoulder and assuring her that it would all be all right, but he couldn't do that. "As much as I want to go for it, I'll admit that I don't see a judge giving anybody a warrant for Garcia's home or his space at work. And I'm not sure what we'd find, anyway. Kids have disappeared in this area out of foster care in the past five years, but we don't have any bodies and there's nothing about the disappearances that makes them stand out."

Kyra's sigh was deep. "Why is it so easy? Every child ought to have somebody that cares about them so much that it would be impossible for them to go missing without an alarm sounding."

"Too bad it doesn't always work that way. You don't have to be in foster care to be ignored, either."

Kyra was silent for a while. "Do you want to talk about it?" she asked softly.

"Not really. I was just thinking about how long my grandparents would have waited to report it if I'd gone missing at sixteen. Probably quite a while. At eighteen it would have taken at least six weeks for them to figure out I was gone because we only communicated about once a month."

"You went back for holidays, though, right?"

Josh shrugged, trying to sound more nonchalant than he felt. "For Christmas break. And the summer after freshman year, but after that I stayed at school and worked jobs there. How about you? You haven't ever said much about your family."

"Not much to tell. I'm an only child and my parents are both living. I was never denied anything money could buy." The narrowing of her eyes and the flattening of her expression told Josh that she wasn't saying any more, either. On the surface it sounded all right, but Josh knew that there was usually a lot more than that in most family situations.

Before he could decide whether or not to dig any deeper today with Kyra, her assistant Allie came into the office. "You've got a phone call on line two. It's Fairfield School. Do you want to take it here or somewhere else?" The young woman looked pointedly in Josh's direction.

"If you'd like, I can step out for a minute." Judging from Allie's crossed arms and brisk tone she thought that would be a good idea.

"No, you don't have to," Kyra said. "Fairfield is where Jasmine goes to school. It's a continuation high school, and unless I'm way off base this call means that she's in trouble again."

Kyra thanked Allie for the warning and picked up the phone on her desk. Josh tried not to listen to the conversation, although he could hear Kyra's tone get more and more agitated. When she put down the phone she sighed and reached into her desk drawer for her purse. "Want to come with me on a scouting mission? Jasmine isn't at school, and isn't at her group home. The social worker at the school wanted to talk to me to make sure Jasmine wasn't with me, because she knows I'm important to her. If Jasmine doesn't show up at school or at the group home in the next four hours they'll have to report her."

"That doesn't sound good. What happens to her at that point?"

"She'd probably go to a stricter, more institutional setting. Knowing Jasmine, that would mean she'd bolt at the first possible opportunity. The thought of that makes my blood run cold. She may act tough but she's not, and she has no resources to live on her own."

"So you're going to see if you can find her?"

Kyra nodded. "I can try. She took the bus to school today, so I have a couple of ideas about where she might be. She has a couple of favorite places."

"Do you think she'll be upset if I go along? I don't want to mess things up even more."

Kyra looked down at her desk, as if weighing the options. "I would like you with me. I really want to make sure Jasmine realizes how serious this is if I find her. Especially if you're right about our killer still being out there. She'd be too attractive a target. Having her go missing would haunt me forever. So please, come with me."

It took about twenty minutes to drive to the area where the school was located. "Continuation schools never get the pretty buildings," Kyra grumbled, passing the worn brick structure. "If I ever come into a lot of money, I'm going to fund the prettiest alternative high school you ever saw."

Her voice sounded wistful and Josh wondered what drove her comment. Somehow he felt it was more than just caring for the girls that she mentored through the church. He didn't have time to pursue the subject further, though, because soon they pulled into the parking lot of a strip mall and Kyra stopped the truck. "I think she'll be in here, either in the used bookstore, the Chinese carryout place or the thrift store. Let's go through them in that order and find out."

There were only two people in the bookstore; the elderly owner and a young man browsing through the science fiction section. Josh was glad they didn't spend much time there because a huge orange tabby cat was stretched out on the front desk, making his nose prickle immediately.

In the farthest booth of the Chinese carryout place, Jasmine sat with a box of fried rice in front of her, engrossed in reading a hardback without a dust jacket. She didn't look up and see them, making it easy for Kyra to sit down at the end of the bench where she sat, blocking her exit. Josh sat down across from the two of them.

"You want to tell me about it?" Kyra said softly.

"Not really." Jasmine glared at her, expression sour. "I really needed a day off from everywhere and everything so I just took it."

"Next time you feel that way, call me. I'll find a way to get you a break without getting you in trouble."

Jasmine's expression didn't change. "Why would you do that?"

"Because I don't want you to die!" Josh jumped along with Jasmine at the intensity of Kyra's statement. "We think there might be somebody out there singling out girls from the system and killing them. Even without that, what you're doing is stupid, and if it goes any further you'll regret it the rest of your life."

"You don't know *anything* about what I'm doing. And you're just trying to scare me with that stuff about a killer. I bet you just don't want a blot on your perfect church-lady record if I run away."

Josh found anger rising in him at Jasmine's hurtful remarks. They'd obviously found their mark with Kyra, because her eyes filled with tears. "I know more than you think about what you're doing," she said softly. Then she did something Josh didn't understand; she pushed up the right sleeve of her soft cotton sweater to show something to Jasmine. It looked like a small tattoo. Josh couldn't tell what it said around a tiny heart. Whatever it was, it made Jasmine's dark eyes go wide as she slumped back against the bench.

"Okay, maybe you do know something. Are you for real about the killer part, too?"

"We're for real," Josh said as Kyra nodded. "Should I leave you two alone to talk for a while?"

"No, stick around. I'm only going to tell this story once and you might as well hear it." Kyra's tone was flat and she stared through him as she folded her hands on the scarred orange laminate surface of the table.

ELEVEN

Kyra hadn't planned to do this with Josh present. What was he going to think of what she had to say? Too late to worry about that now. He seemed to sense her discomfort. "Do you want me to leave?" he asked softly.

She shook her head, then angled her body slightly toward Jasmine. "No, but I know my throat's going to get dry. Could you get me something to drink? Diet soda is fine."

He slid out of the booth and went up to the counter. Jasmine looked down at Kyra's arm again and reached out to trace the small pink heart tattoo. She let her, not even flinching when she felt Jasmine's soft finger on her skin. "How old were you?"

She didn't have to ask anything more. Kyra couldn't deny what Jasmine had understood immediately. "I was two months short of my seventeenth birthday when my daughter was born. She lived three days."

"I'm sorry. Was she sick?" Kyra noticed that Jasmine's hand went unconsciously to her midsection, protectively curving around the top of her rounded belly.

"She was premature, and there were some other problems, too." In her mind's eye, Kyra could see the tiny incubator in the neonatal intensive-care unit, hear the beeping and whooshing all around her from those days in the NICU. The lights had always been on there, day and night. You couldn't tell what time it was or what day it was.

Jasmine still looked at Kyra's arm, her eyes filling with tears now. "Lissa Rose was her name? Is that for anybody in your family?"

"The Rose was for my gran who raised me." Just saying her name put another picture in Kyra's mind, of the compact, sweet woman with soft hands and brown hair streaked with silver. "She had the same blue eyes that Lissa did when she was born."

On the table a plastic cup of soda with a red straw poking through the lid had appeared by her elbow. Kyra took a sip, letting the cold liquid sting a little on the back of her throat. Jasmine's eyes searched her face. "Your gran, was she there when you had the baby?"

"No. She died two years before that, a sudden stroke nobody expected. When that happened I thought maybe my parents would take me back and I'd live with them, but a week after the funeral they shipped me off to a girls' school. I lasted a month there before I left." The pictures in her mind now weren't comforting. Kyra knew she didn't have to spell things out for Jasmine, because the teen had been on the streets herself. It wasn't a welcoming place for a girl of fourteen and they both knew that.

Kyra leaned back against the hard surface of the rigid booth seat and took another drink of cold soda. Josh sat across from them, quiet and pale. His voice was the next one to break the silence. "How long did it take them to find you?"

Kyra shrugged. "They didn't look real hard. I found out later they filed reports with the police, but they didn't hire a private detective or anything. After eight months or so I got picked up for shoplifting and spent some time in the juvenile justice system."

Jasmine was still wide-eyed. "I am *not* believing this. You're smart, Miss Kyra. Why did you do something so…?"

"Stupid?" Kyra supplied the missing word. "Because I was a rebellious, angry teenager positive nobody in the world loved me or cared about me. And it felt like my parents were proving that, because when I got done with my time for shoplifting they picked me up and got ready to take me back to that school again. When I said I wouldn't go back they pretty much wrote me off. They gave me money and told me that until I wanted to do things their way I was on my own."

Kyra could hear Josh gasp. She didn't look at him, not sure she could continue her story if she looked and saw pity on his face. So she kept her focus on Jasmine and went on. "So did you get your own place? Was it cool doing what you wanted?" Jasmine's expression showed she was hungry to hear certain answers, but the tentative way she asked told Kyra that she already knew what had happened.

"What do you think?" Kyra asked her softly. "When you left the last time, how did it work out for you?"

Jasmine sighed. "I told myself it didn't work out because I didn't have any money. I guess from what you're saying it didn't work out for you, either, even with the money, huh?"

"It didn't. I made some really stupid decisions, like hanging out with the wrong people and partying a lot. Six months later I had to admit that I was broke, pregnant and alone." Kyra couldn't meet Josh's startled look. "I had no idea what to do next and when I called them my parents wanted nothing to do with me."

"Where did you go?" Jasmine leaned forward in her seat.

"Somebody told me about Covenant House and it saved my life." Kyra could still remember walking into the shabby brick building the first time, wondering what a bunch of Christian hypocrites could possibly do for her. By the end of the day they'd taken her in and found a bed for her. By the end of the week she'd had a full medical checkup, her first in years. She was eating nutritious meals and sleeping in a clean bed, the same one every night. When she wasn't working, she could study. It felt like heaven. "I couldn't understand why anybody would do what these people did, when nobody else wanted me. They explained that God still wanted me, a lot. And I believed them."

"Were you afraid?" Kyra knew what Jasmine was asking, and she nodded, unable to say anything more for a moment. Breathing a silent prayer for strength and guidance, she gathered herself and took another sip from her drink.

"I was really scared. Especially about a month into my stay there when I felt awful and everything hurt and I ended up in the hospital having my baby, way too early. One of the counselors from Covenant House stayed with me all the time for two days. Her name was Melissa, and that's where the Lissa part of Lissa Rose's name came from."

"Do you still think God wants you? Aren't you mad that He took Lissa?" Kyra had heard that question before and by now she'd had almost thirteen years to work on her answer.

"I know God wants me, and he wants Josh and he wants you. God's just crazy in love with each one of us, and that's why Jesus came and lived and died and rose. For us, each one of us. And I don't think God 'took' Lissa any more than I think God 'took' the victims of the killer I'm trying to protect you from."

"Then what happened?" This time it was Josh with the question, leaning forward against the table as urgently as Jasmine. This was another question Kyra worked on for a long time, and she tried to put the answer into words that both of her friends could understand.

"Life happened, and my God-given free will to make really lousy choices happened. I was living out on the streets, drinking and barely surviving. Taking care of myself because I was going to have a baby was the last thing on my mind. In fact, I denied the reality of that as long as possible."

"So you blame yourself for your daughter's death?"

Josh's second question stung a bit, and it took a minute for Kyra to realize that he'd reached over the table and grasped her hand gently. "I have to at least take responsibility for my poor choices. Of course I wasn't the only one who made some bad moves. My parents weren't right when they cut me out of their lives, and that led to some of my problems. If you want to start with blame that can go on forever. When I was seventeen and dealing with losing my baby it was easy to fall into blame. But twelve years later I'm in a different place and usually blame is a waste of time."

Josh didn't have much expression on his lean face. "Okay. I guess I can see that. What about the rest of us who aren't in that place yet? What are we supposed to do?"

From her right Kyra saw Jasmine nodding. "Yeah. I get that running away now would be a bad choice. But what am I supposed to do instead? I hate the place I'm staying and it's hard to feel like anybody, even God, cares about me there." Her thin shoulders sagged and Kyra slipped her hand out from Josh's grasp so that she could put an arm around the girl.

"Let's go someplace else and talk a little more and pray some. I really want to do that. Is that okay with you?"

Jasmine pushed her plate away. "I guess. Where do you want to go?"

Kyra looked at Jasmine as she tried to figure out whether or not the idea growing in her mind was the best one she'd had in a long time, or the absolute worst. "Let's go back to my office. Then I'll take you back to school before the last bell."

Kyra could tell that both Jasmine and Josh wanted to argue with her, but neither actually did. So they went out to her pickup and found room for the three of them on the bench seat. All the way to the lab she prayed. *Please, Lord, let me be doing the right thing.*

The ride back to the lab was extremely quiet. Josh spent the time wondering what he should say to Kyra. Her story had ripped a hole in his heart and he literally ached for her. This was the woman he'd assumed had a smooth and easy life? Right now he didn't even understand how she'd stayed sane, much less as calm and happy as she appeared most of the time.

He looked over to the driver's seat where she concentrated on the road, brow slightly furrowed. He wasn't so sure that taking Jasmine back to the lab was such a great idea. He didn't know enough about teen girls to really argue; for all he knew this could be exactly the wake-up call she needed.

Right now she sat between them, and Josh could feel the sharp bones of her elbow or shoulder occasionally as Kyra's pickup bounced over a bump. Her hands in her lap fiddled nervously with her seat belt, worn low to accommodate the growing child within. With a start Josh realized that the young girl next to him was only slightly older than Chrissie had been when he'd left for college. They'd never lived under the same

roof and hadn't developed any kind of real relationship as adults.

Watching Jasmine gave Josh a pang of regret that
he'd missed so much of his sister's life. She was the
only person on the planet who remembered some of
the same things he did, knew some of the same stories.
He promised himself that once he got home tonight he
would gather up all of those Christmas cards and get
online and find out all about the town in Iowa where
Chrissie and her husband and kids lived. Then he'd
search out any phone numbers he could find for her
and make that call he should have made years ago.
What if she hung up on him? No, that was getting
ahead of himself. First he had to find a phone number
and work up some courage.

The truck stopping in the lot drew Josh back to the
present and reality. Tonight he could start the hunt for
Chrissie. Right now he needed to go into the building
with Kyra and Jasmine and see what would happen there.

He found himself carrying on a silent running dia-
logue. Only after a few minutes, walking through the
parking lot, did he realize that this was prayer. He was
talking to God, asking for peace for himself, for Kyra
and for this troubled young girl. He asked for guidance
to help Kyra do the right thing. The glass doors of the
building whooshed open as they walked in and Josh
continued praying silently. So this was what a conversation with God felt like. He'd started something like
this back in his car before he'd ever come to the lab,
but at that point God felt pretty far away.

This conversation was different and Josh knew that God wasn't the one who had changed. He'd started to read the Bible that Kyra had given him, and last night he'd gotten to a part that said God was the same yesterday, today and tomorrow. They were back to the lab now, and once they got Jasmine settled and sitting down, Josh motioned to Kyra and they stepped through the door just outside Kyra's office.

"So, what's up? How much are you going to show her? I have to tell you that I'd argue against going in there with the gurneys."

Kyra shook her head. "Don't worry. I considered that at first and rejected it. I've been praying about it most of the way here."

"So have I," Josh admitted, enjoying seeing Kyra's eyes widen. "Yeah, I thought that would surprise you."

She grinned wryly. "It shouldn't, but you caught me. That's a good thing. So what were you praying for?"

"It's so new a feeling that it's hard for me to describe. For strength, I guess, and guidance, and for knowing what's the right thing to do in this situation."

Kyra nodded. "And apparently prayer led us to the same conclusion. I don't want to show Jasmine those bones, but I do want her to know how serious this all is. So I'm going to pull the file pictures that we have and walk through them with her. I'll explain how hard it was to get to this point where we actually know who these people really were." She smiled slightly. "I'd appreciate it if you hung around. If things get too hard for you to handle, let me know and we'll find a way for you to go somewhere else for a while, okay?"

"Sounds okay to me. Now, let's go back before that kid has a panic attack or starts opening things she shouldn't in the office."

"Right. I hate to ask you for this kind of help again, but could you go scout us up a couple of bottles of water? You know where they are in the break fridge. That way I can start the talk with Jasmine."

Josh nodded in agreement and went to the break room while Kyra went back around the corner to her office. When he came back with the water she'd asked for, Jasmine already had a box of tissues right in front of her. "She's younger than me, isn't she?" she asked in a small voice, running an index fingertip along the photo of Nikki.

"Right. She never got past fourteen and her story sounds a lot like yours. Her family was too messed up to deal with her, and she bounced around in the system a lot. She spent a while at Diane and Gary's. That's how we figured out who she was, because Diane still had some of her things. We might never have known otherwise, because after almost eight years, all that was left were bones and a few cloth scraps. That's not enough by itself to identify a human being."

Jasmine shuddered, and Josh felt like going to her and putting an arm around her thin shoulders to tell her it was going to be all right. Instead he put the water bottles down on Kyra's desk and went back to sit in his chair nearby. "Do you know how she died?" Jasmine's voice stayed soft and tentative, without the tough veneer she usually wore.

"There's nothing obvious on the bones we found, like evidence of a gunshot or a knife wound. The only other bone that would probably tell us how she was killed would be a small bone in the neck called the hyoid bone, and we didn't find that in any of the three victims we discovered together."

"Three?" Jasmine squeaked. "You mean she wasn't alone?"

"She was alone when she died, except for whoever killed her," Josh said. "But we found evidence of three bodies together out in the woods."

Kyra started setting the pictures in front of Jasmine. "This is Gen. She was eighteen, and this picture is her with her son, Andre. He was two when she disappeared and he's in fourth grade now." She looked over at Josh and gave him a slight nod, which he answered back.

She put the next picture down and he moved his chair closer to her desk. "This is Serita. She was just about your age. What they all three had in common is that they were in the foster care system, or they had been, and they'd run away or gone from placement to placement."

"We think that's one of the reasons the killer was attracted to them. He seemed to think they wouldn't be missed nearly as quickly, so they were fair game. The thing of it was that he was right."

"That's not fair." Jasmine's voice was almost a whisper. "Somebody should have cared about them."

"Somebody did, but nobody was determined enough to keep looking for them once they disappeared. Even though it wasn't right or fair, they fell through the cracks and someone got away with murder at least three times."

"Probably more," Josh added. "What I've seen makes me think there are more victims. And killers like this don't stop unless they're dead or in prison."

Jasmine slumped in her chair. "This is why you got so upset when I ditched school today, huh? You must think this guy is still out there."

"This is why Miss Kyra wants you to stick to the rules for a while. If you don't make yourself a target, you'll stay safer."

Kyra reached over her desk and put a hand on the girl's thin arm. "Can we take you back now? And will you agree to stay there? I care about you, Jasmine, but I can't keep you safe all the time. You need to stick to the rules even if you don't like it."

"You know I don't like it. I never have any privacy and somebody's always after me for something. Are you sure I can't stay with you, just for a couple of weeks?"

Josh watched Kyra as she struggled with her answer. "We've talked about this before, and you know what I said then. I work too much and I live too far from your school for me to be approved as even a temporary guardian. Besides, with the personal record I told you about today, it's unlikely I could get approved even if everything else worked out."

Josh could see Jasmine's lower lip trembling. "But

you're an important person with a good life. Why would they care what happened to you when you were my age?"

"For the same reason when you're my age, your employer and the important people in your life, will care about what you did as a teenager," Kyra said simply. "What you do now will impact who you become. That's probably reason number two that I want you to go back to your group home and play by the rules for a little while. Not only do I want you to stay safe, but I want you to plan for the future."

Jasmine shrugged slightly, lifting one shoulder. "That's all so far away if seems silly to do that."

"Maybe so. All I can tell you is the way I see it, and how I feel. Sometimes it feels like it was only yesterday that I watched Lissa Rose die in front of me. And she'd be almost a teenager if she were still here. If I hadn't started planning before she was born I wouldn't be where I am today. I might not have gone to college or on to grad school. I know I wouldn't have discovered just what it is that God wants me to do with my life."

Jasmine stayed silent for a short time, regarding Kyra with a thoughtful expression. "Are you doing it, do you think? Is this where God wants you to be?"

"Yes, I think it is. And as much as you hate to hear it, I think going back to the group home and taking care of yourself and that baby would be what God wants you to do."

Jasmine grimaced. "I know you're right, but I hate to hear it. Let's go before I change my mind again."

* * *

All the time Kyra was gone with Jasmine, Josh worked on reports having to do with the case. It was slow going because his mind was on Kyra and what she'd said earlier. He kept hearing her words about Lissa Rose. Every time they echoed he wanted to kick himself for being such an idiot. No wonder she'd reacted the way she had when he said she'd had an easy life. She'd had anything but ease and still she'd gone on to be a compassionate and skilled forensic anthropologist. He was beginning to understand what she said about "call," too. Not that he had any idea what something like that would be like for him, but believing that Kyra was called to what she did made sense.

She'd be back in the office anytime and he'd have to face her. That was the last thing Josh wanted to do right now. He felt so transparent that Kyra would know with one look that he was in love with her. Then she'd tell him what she thought of him and he wouldn't be able to fool himself anymore. Their time together was going to be short, anyway; no sense in making it short and painful. Shutting down his computer and packing his briefcase, he left and made the trip home in silence, wondering what on earth he should do next.

TWELVE

Josh was gone when Kyra got back. That told her everything she needed to know. Josh had heard her story and had not said a word to her afterward about how he felt. He'd looked strained and angry, but at the time she'd blamed it on his trying to protect Jasmine when he thought that she was going to take the girl into the back room. Now she wasn't so sure. Maybe he had been repelled by her story. For Jasmine's sake she hadn't glossed anything over, although she hadn't gone into details on the worst of her choices during that dark time in her life.

Jasmine hadn't asked much about Kyra's parents, and for that she was thankful. She still didn't communicate with them all that much. After her father retired from the international conglomerate that had taken them around the globe, they'd settled in a small town in upstate New York. Technically they were just a few hours away, but given their differences it might as well be another planet. No matter what Kyra did with her life her parents wouldn't forgive her for the embarrassment they'd suffered when she ran away. Even before that they hadn't really known what to do with a teenager; after that they didn't want anything to do with her.

Her parents had never been people of faith, and her choice to become a Christian had confused them more than anything else about her journey into adulthood. She'd gone to church with Gran as a child, but fallen away from that as a teen, until she'd gotten so far from those roots that she felt alone and abandoned. Then when things were the absolute worst, she felt God's love surround her again, even though she couldn't imagine how anybody would want to care about her.

Now she couldn't imagine how she'd get through life without faith. When things were good she had somewhere to share her joy, and when they were bad she laid her sorrows at the foot of the cross. This was going to be a big burden to put there, Kyra thought. Until now she thought that maybe she and Josh were coming together, making some progress. Now it was clear that she'd been wrong. She got her office in order as much as possible and headed out a little early for a change. She knew she'd be in during the weekend. Maybe for once she'd rent a movie and enjoy just vegging out. "It's not going to be a romantic comedy," she muttered, heading for the parking lot.

By Monday morning Kyra was more than ready to go back to work. She hadn't had a single phone call all weekend, and once she'd left the store where she'd rented her DVDs, she hadn't even spoken with another human being until church on Sunday morning. All day

Saturday she'd cleaned the house, given Ranger plenty of attention, cooked dinner and treated herself to a long soak in a hot tub.

By Sunday evening she'd watched all the movies she cared to see, finished up the stack of professional journals that tended to pile up on her nightstand, and done everything but alphabetized the spices in the pantry. Even Josh was a welcome sight on Monday morning when he came into the office about forty-five minutes after she did.

"Hey. Thanks for making coffee. I didn't stop anywhere to get some on the way in to work." He put down his briefcase at his workstation and poured himself a mug of coffee.

"Hey yourself," Kyra answered back. "How was your weekend?"

"Okay, I guess." He didn't offer any details and Kyra didn't feel like pressing. In fact, she didn't feel much like keeping a conversation going without help. If Josh didn't want to volunteer anything, she wasn't going to force him. Was the silence that settled between them the way things were going to be for this last week or two that Josh spent in her office? Kyra hoped not, but she didn't know how to break the tension.

They both worked quietly at their computers for a while. Kyra was catching up on the incredible amount of paperwork she'd let slide in the past two weeks while she'd concentrated on finding the identities of the three young women in the lab. After a second cup of coffee and a couple of trips back and forth to the printer in the next room, Josh packed up papers in his brief-case, leaving the computer still set up and other papers on the desk. "So what's up for you today?" she asked.

"I still don't have enough to bug you about getting any kind of warrant on Garcia, but I want to talk to him. I have some plausible questions about Nikki and Gen, and a few on one of the other missing girls we haven't found any sign of."

Kyra eyed him sharply. "Are you sure you can talk to him without giving anything away? If you're right and he's the guy, I don't have to tell you what kind of repercussions there'd be if he got scared off."

"Don't worry. I can handle talking to Garcia. Mess-ing up something this basic would put the final nail in the coffin of my career, and I'm not ready for that. I'll be back in a couple of hours, that or I'll call in if things get more complicated. How about you? What's the rest of your morning like?"

Kyra shrugged. "More paperwork, I imagine. And then I'll be documenting the remains in the next room one more time, so that in any eventual trial no one can say that the state forensics experts were anything but meticulous. Whether or not Garcia is the one who did this, I don't want the killer going free some day on any technicality involving my office."

"Sounds reasonable to me. I'll see you later."

"Later," Kyra echoed, watching him leave. She held back a sigh. Nothing that they'd said to each other all morning was personal or friendly. Josh had kept every-thing on a business level, although Kyra had to admit that she had as well. Still, she'd been holding out the hope that he would come in today and they'd talk about Friday and what she'd said about her life. She was surer than ever that Josh was ready to go back to the FBI and never see her again. The thought gave her a sad, hollow feeling.

The phone on the desk rang, startling her a little. The number on the caller ID was all too familiar and she felt a flash of anger. After everything she'd said on Friday, how could Jasmine possibly have cut classes today or walked out of school? It was the only reason for the attendance office there to be calling.

"She was here for her first-hour class," the attendance clerk told Kyra. "But nobody remembers seeing her after that except one girl who said she 'might' have seen Jasmine leave and head for the bus stop across the street."

Kyra sighed in earnest this time, unable to hold back her disappointment. "Great. Have you alerted her placement manager yet? I guess you have to this time."

"I thought I'd call you first, but if you haven't heard anything, this time I've got to go through channels."

"Go ahead. I'm not in the business of rescuing people from themselves." They exchanged a few more words and Kyra put down the phone, her eyes filling with tears. Jasmine had really seemed to get it on Friday. How could she possibly do this only two days later?

Kyra sat silently at her desk, praying for comfort and clarity for herself and for guidance and safety for Jasmine. Shaking her head, she went back to her paperwork. A few minutes later the ringing of her cell phone startled her out of her contemplation of a complicated report.

"Miss Kyra? I need help. I did something dumb and now I don't feel good and I'm scared and…well, I just need help."

"Okay, slow down," Kyra told Jasmine, whose voice was higher and more childlike than usual. "First tell me why you don't feel good and where you are. Do we need to call 911?"

"Maybe. No, I don't think so. That means an ambulance or cops or something and I don't feel that bad. Can you come get me? I'm about six blocks from my school sitting in front of that burned-out place on Washington that you told me was a crack house."

"The place I specifically told you to stay as far away as possible from?"

There was a long pause. "Yeah. That one. Anyway, I still need you to come get me. If I call school or my placement counselor I'll get in even more trouble than I'm already in. Please, Miss Kyra?"

"All right, but be prepared, because I can't get you out of the trouble you're in. Go to the nearest business that's open and wait there for me. I can be there in about fifteen minutes."

"I'll wait for you." Jasmine's answer was a little less hysterical, and now Kyra didn't feel as anxious herself.

She grabbed her purse and her other essentials and scribbled a quick note to Josh on a sticky notepad, taking the sheet when she was done and attaching it squarely on his computer screen where he couldn't miss it. Then, praying all the while, she got into her truck and started heading toward the block of downtrodden row houses where she prayed that Jasmine would wait for her the way she said she would.

Josh sat in the waiting room of the clinic as patients filled the plastic chairs around him. A couple of small children played with blocks that had seen better days, while another little guy sat on his mom's lap looking too miserable to join them. Ramon Garcia came out with a clipboard and scanned the people. "Simmons," he barked, impatient for an answer. "Simmons. Travis Simmons."

The woman with the sick toddler hoisted him off her lap as he protested, and stood up with him in her arms. She walked toward Garcia, who reached out as if to take the child, who reacted with a wail.

"I'm going in there with him," the woman said firmly.

"He'll cry more if you do. They always put on a show for the parents," Garcia snapped. "And I don't have all day to do this."

"I'm going in there with him," she repeated, staring down the medical technician. He had to outweigh her by fifty pounds and was at least six inches taller, but she had a mother's determination.

Finally Garcia shrugged and turned on his heel. "Fine," he said without looking back. "But if I can't get this done in five minutes, that's it. I can't mess up the whole day's schedule because you won't calm down your kid."

"He's been throwing up for two days and running a fever," the woman said softly to the man's retreating back. She followed him into the treatment room and the door slammed behind them. Josh could almost feel steam coming out of his ears at Garcia's attitude with her. She was worried about her sick child, and if he'd been as sick as she described, it probably meant that she hadn't slept the past two nights. Of course she wasn't going to hand him off to some stranger.

Not only was he rude and brusque with his patients, he didn't even tell them the truth. The clinic manager had already told Josh that Garcia had at least forty-five minutes between patients once this appointment was over, and there he was telling this mom that he had five minutes to complete her child's test or he'd toss them out.

Josh had to remind himself that simply being unpleasant didn't make Garcia a serial killer. True, they were probably looking for somebody who didn't deal well with other people, but that wasn't everything. Many people lied and way too many of them were rude. Those types had been part of his daily routine not that long ago. Since he'd started working with Kyra, he'd begun to notice how much better most people reacted to the truth and a little bit of common courtesy. Now, that didn't mean he'd act that way with every suspect and lowlife he came in contact with, but he could always try.

Ten minutes later Travis and his mom and Garcia came out of the treatment room. "Go to the main desk and talk to them about an appointment for results. And good luck to you."

Okay, that was a surprise. Ramon was actually being a regular guy for once. Maybe he had an idea of who Josh was and decided to put on a front. Or maybe he could actually be a regular guy when he put his mind to it.

Josh stood and went back to the doorway of the treatment room. "Ramon Garcia? Josh Richards. I need a few minutes of your time."

"What if I don't want to give it to you?" Okay, so he wasn't a regular guy all the time.

"Then we can go back to the state police building where I have my office and talk there."

Garcia held up a hand. "Whoa, no need for that. Come in and shut the door, Mr...."

"Richards. Agent Richards." Josh closed the door and went to the small desk in the corner where Garcia sat. He took a seat in the plastic chair that served as a side chair. "I'm here investigating the disappearance of several young women whose bodies have recently been identified. One of their common links was being treated in this clinic. Specifically, most of them came through that door into this room." Josh spread the pictures of Gen, Serita and Nikki out on the desk. He'd added Lisa Phipps's picture as well in hopes of tripping Garcia up. She fit the general profile and she was still missing.

Garcia's eyes held no light. "Agent Richards, do you have any idea how many people come through that door every week? A hundred or more. That means about three thousand a year. Now, I know from people talking around here that these kids you're talking about have been missing something like seven or eight years. How do you expect me to remember that far back?"

Josh would have believed him if Garcia's gaze hadn't strayed back to the photos at least twice during his speech. "Try a little harder. This one's Gen," he said, pushing her photo forward with one finger. "And she told a friend that a guy was going to get her a job, a good job. In the medical field. Funny, the name she gave her friend sounded a lot like yours."

Garcia continued to stare at the picture. "Her, I remember. Not the name, but the second part. The last time I saw her she was bringing a kid in, maybe for a hearing test because of ear infections. She told me that somebody was going to help her get a job like mine. I asked her if that somebody told her that she was going to need at least two years of school to do that, and she said no. I tried to tell her that it was a scam and that the guy wanted something from her, but she didn't want to listen."

Josh was so stunned that he couldn't speak. While he tried to form the next question Garcia surprised him even more. "And I remember this one, too." He separated out the photo of Lisa Phipps. "She asked if I could do a test for her without telling anybody. She said she'd pay cash and we could just keep it a secret."

"What kind of test?" Josh leaned forward to hear the answer.

"A pregnancy test. I told her that I couldn't do something like that for anybody, and especially not a minor.

I told her she needed to talk to somebody about this, like maybe her case manager or somebody she trusted."

Garcia looked Josh straight in the eye and this time his dark eyes held the expression Josh had looked for before. "She said there wasn't anybody she could trust. Too bad, because she looked like an okay kid, and maybe fourteen at most. Kids that young, there should be somebody they trust."

The room seemed to spin around Josh. He felt as if he'd been hit by a wrecking ball. Garcia was telling the truth. There were too many things in his statement that would have incriminated him otherwise. No one was as good an actor as you'd have to be to say what he just had and lie through all of it.

Garcia was not their guy. Josh was beginning to get an idea who might be, though, and he needed to talk to Kyra. "Would you tell all this to somebody from the district attorney's office?"

There was silence for a moment, then Garcia leaned back in his office chair, making it groan. "Yeah, I guess. Nobody should get away with murder, and if you think this will help, I'll do it."

"Good. I'll make sure the right person calls you in the next seven days." Josh gathered up his things and headed for the door as quickly as possible. He was barely through the waiting room and out the door before he called Kyra. There was no answer on her cell or on the work phone, either. He began to get a very bad feeling about everything, and struggled to push it away. He prayed all the way back to the office.

When he got back there he searched quickly through the office and the labs, but Kyra wasn't there. Neither was Allie, and for a few minutes Josh held out the hope that maybe they'd just gone to lunch together. Just to make sure, he picked up the receiver of Kyra's phone and punched the buttons to see the last few incoming calls. His heart sank when he saw the last one. He scrolled all the way back to Friday and found the same number with the same ID for Jasmine's school.

Replacing the phone on Kyra's desk, he paced through the department one last time. When he got to the room where most of the staff had their desks and cubicles, Allie stood next to hers hanging a damp jacket on a hook. "Where's Kyra?" he asked, trying to keep the panic out of his voice.

"Isn't she back yet? She said she was going after Jasmine, but that she'd be back soon." Allie pressed her lips together in an expression of worry. "That was at least twenty minutes before I went to lunch. I thought she'd get here before I did."

"She's not here. And I didn't see her truck in the lot, but I was trying to tell myself that she'd just parked in a different area," Josh admitted. "Did she say where she was going after Jasmine?"

"No, she just said she was very unhappy with her because she was where she shouldn't be. Apparently the kid called her from someplace after she ditched school this morning."

The hair on the back of Josh's neck prickled. "Call

the detective unit and tell a supervisor everything you just told me, and tell them we have reason to believe that someone has abducted Kyra and Jasmine."

Allie took a step backward. "We do?"

"Yeah, we do." Josh picked up a notepad from her desk and started writing on it. "And tell them that I've gone to this address to try to figure out where the two of them are. I'll call when I find something out."

"Okay." Allie still looked puzzled, but Josh saw that she was already punching numbers in the phone as he turned to leave.

He broke all kinds of traffic laws on his way to his destination, but naturally there wasn't a police unit of any kind that pulled him over. He got to the Griffith household in record time, parking his car in front of the house as quickly as possible and taking the short flight of stairs to the door two at a time.

Diana Griffith answered his heavy knock quickly. "You're the investigator who was here with Dr. Elliott. Did you forget to ask me something before?"

"Not exactly, but I don't think we want to discuss what I have to say on the doorstep. May I come in?"

"I guess so. Follow me back to the kitchen because I'm in the middle of the home-from-school rush. The grade-schoolers are upstairs doing homework and I need to get ready for the older kids coming home."

Josh thanked her and followed Diana to the back of the house. He felt so nervous that he had to wipe the palms of his hands on his pants. *Please, Lord, let me be wrong,* he prayed silently. But in his heart he already knew that now, too late, he had the right answer to what had happened directly under their noses.

THIRTEEN

The last time he'd been here, Josh enjoyed the atmosphere in Diana's homey kitchen. Now every muscle was taut and he could barely keep from yelling. "Have you heard from your husband today?" he asked her, hoping he was wrong and she could prove that.

"A few hours ago. He called and said he had to do something off-site and he wouldn't be home until very late tonight." She gave Josh an assessing look, as if she wondered whether to say more or not.

"What else did you want to tell me?" Josh tried to keep his voice even and calm.

Diana paused a moment more. "Well, this isn't going to sound like something that should concern me, but it did. Gary told me he loved me, and he told me to tell Sarah that as well."

"And that's unusual for him?" Josh already knew the answer, and his heart sank to the level of his knees.

"Very unusual. Gary just isn't the demonstrative type. He's solid, dependable, but not the kind of guy who's romantic or mushy."

"Have you and Gary ever had…difficulties…in your marriage? I'm not coming out of the blue with this," he said at her worried look. "I'm trying to decide whether I need to involve you and your husband more deeply in our investigation. Honestly, I'm hoping for every reason not to, because we've got something extremely serious going on."

Diana's dark eyes filled with tears. "Around the time that Sarah was born things got sort of odd for us. Gary was distant and angry a lot, and he stayed that way through her infancy. And when Sarah was less than a year old he lost his grandmother, who raised him, and I put our problems down to that and being a new dad."

"You lived in this area then?"

Diana nodded. "We were managing another group home about four miles from here. Then when Sarah was a toddler we moved here and we've been here ever since." She looked down at the table in front of her, and then looked up with troubled eyes. "There's something very wrong, isn't there?"

"I'm afraid so. I think that a young woman who was one of your foster kids at one point has been abducted by your husband. And I'm really worried that she was taken to lure Kyra into a trap."

Diana choked back a sob. "Part of me wants to scream that what you're saying isn't possible. That my husband could never be involved in something like that. But I can't be sure. Gary's not…well…and I don't think he's been following up on doctor's visits and medication lately. And several times lately I've woken up in the middle of the night and he wasn't in our room." She looked out the windows, as if to make sure they weren't being watched. "He wasn't even in the house. When I asked him about it, he said he'd been taking long walks to clear his head. It's the same kind of thing he did when Sarah was a baby."

Josh could feel his palms sweat while his mouth was cotton dry with fear. "Does Gary have access to any weapons? And can you think of anywhere he would be likely to go if he wanted to hide something?"

"He's a hospital security guard, so he has plenty of access to weapons. You probably didn't know that because I make him leave his uniform at work, along with his gun, so he doesn't upset the kids. But as far as places he'd go, I have no idea."

"I know, Mommy." Sarah's small voice came from the doorway.

Josh frowned, wondering how long she'd been there listening. He looked at Diana, wondering what to do next. He didn't really want to involve a second-grader in this kind of business, but on the other hand he wanted to hear what she had to say."

"What do you mean, Sarah-bug?" Diana tried to sound light, sitting down in a kitchen chair and motioning for her daughter to come into the room. The child did, climbing up on her mother's lap.

"You know how Daddy is always saying I'm his favorite girl in the whole wide world? I think that's silly, because I'm his only little girl, but he thinks it's funny because he smiles. Sometimes when we go out for ice cream on Saturdays he takes me someplace else after that. One place he calls his secret garden, but last week he said we couldn't go there anymore because somebody dug it up." Her brow furrowed and she looked up at her mother. "Why would somebody do that, dig up somebody else's garden?"

Josh had to sit down on one of the other kitchen chairs. He couldn't trust his knees to hold him up any longer. "That sounds mean, doesn't it?" Sarah nodded. "You said that one place was what he called his garden, Sarah. Is there another place?"

"Yeah, but I don't like it. One time a spider got in my hair. Daddy says spiders aren't scary and they live in barns, anyway, and we shouldn't kill them. I told him that the spiders could have that old barn because I didn't want to go there, anyway."

"How far away was this barn? Did you drive there?" Josh tried hard to keep from sounding harsh with the child. She might be the only link to finding Jasmine and Kyra while they were still alive.

Sarah looked up at her mother's face again, and Diana silently urged her to go on. "I don't know how far it was because I fell asleep on the way there. Daddy said his nana had horses there a long time ago. Does that help?"

"It helps a lot, sweetheart," Diana told her. "Now, why don't you go upstairs and finish your homework, okay?"

"Okay. But if you go to that barn, watch out for spiders," Sarah told Josh.

"I will," he promised, then stayed silent until they

could hear her going up the stairs. "Does that give you an idea of where this place might be?"

"Yes. Gary's grandmother lived out in the more rural part of Frederick County. She didn't own a lot of property, but I do remember going for a drive with her a long time ago and her pointing out a farmstead she said belonged to a good friend."

"Could you find it again?"

"I think so. I could probably narrow it down on a map for you, but it would be a lot easier if I just went with you. I'll need to find someone to watch Sarah and the other kids."

Josh hesitated. "I don't want to involve you in this, especially since all of this could be a wild-goose chase." He didn't really believe that, but involving civilians in something like this when a family member was a suspect was never a good idea.

"Please. I promise, once we find the place you can take me somewhere out of the way. I don't want to be there, anyway, if I'm right."

Josh made a quick decision. "All right. But I'm going to hold you to your word on taking you somewhere else and quickly if we find Gary there. Now, do you have a map in the house that would show that area, or should I go out to the car?"

"I've got one," Diana said, leaving the kitchen and coming back a few minutes later with a map of the area. "I need to call a friend to come and be here for the kids. I need somebody over twenty-one to be in charge."

Josh nodded and studied the map while she made a

couple of calls. He used his own phone to call back to the lab and reach Allie, giving her the information so that troopers could meet them at a main intersection. By the time he'd finished his call, Diana was standing in the kitchen doorway with Sarah. The girl had both fists wrapped in the hem of her mother's sweater. "She's not going to let us leave her behind," Diana said, sounding exhausted. "If you want me, you're going to have to take both of us."

It was against everything that Josh had ever learned, but he knew they were probably running out of time. "Come on, then. We've only got a few more hours of daylight to find this place."

Kyra's arms ached and her head hurt. Every time the van hit a bump she jostled against Jasmine, usually making her whimper. When she'd found the teen sitting on a bus stop bench a few doors down from the crack house, she'd looked small sitting next to a stranger who sat reading the newspaper. His tweed cap had been pulled low over his eyes, and as Kyra got out of her car and crossed the street she had wondered why Jasmine wasn't standing up to meet her.

Once she got within a few steps of the bench she could see why. The man's left wrist and Jasmine's right one were cuffed together with plastic restraints like the state troopers used for temporary handcuffs. Reaching his right arm over his body, behind the paper he now let drop, the man held a stiletto-thin blade to Jasmine's midsection. "Do what I say, stay quiet, or she dies right here. I'm fast with this. If you scream, she and the baby will go in one thrust." Jasmine's eyes were huge with fear and Kyra stood frozen, dumbly wondering why she'd left her cell phone in the car and why the three of them seemed to be the only people around.

The man's voice was familiar, but his taut face and wild eyes weren't...until she'd stood there another long minute. "Gary? What's going on? Why are you doing this?"

"Because it's time. I couldn't stop the urges anymore and she wouldn't stop staring at me. Her and the rest of them." He got to his feet, wrenching Jasmine along. "Come on. Walk over there to that white van. Now."

Kyra wanted to scream or run or do anything that could save the two of them from getting anywhere near that van. She knew the cardinal rule with dangerous people was not to let them get you alone, or let them control you. But Jasmine gasped and a tiny flower of red bloomed on her shirt. "I said move and I mean it." He motioned with his head to the van and Kyra walked to the van. "Now, open the back." Her nerves screamed silently, but she did what he told her to, conscious of Jasmine's terror.

"I don't want to die," the girl said in a tiny voice, hardly more than a whisper.

"Then you'll do what I tell you." He was too close to Kyra for comfort, but before she could shift or move he'd leaned against her, blocking her from moving away from the open hatch of the van. He pushed her and she felt a sharp jab, blaming it on the knife until she looked down between them and saw a needle in Gary's hand instead. "Relax," he said with a sneer. "It's not anything fatal. You'll probably be out only a few minutes. Working at a hospital has some advantages."

That was the last she'd been aware of until coming to with her face pressed against the carpet of a moving vehicle. Now she wasn't sure how long they'd been traveling, but what little she could see out of the darkened windows hinted at rural areas.

Another bounce rocked her against Jasmine, who made a high-pitched sob. "Are you hurt?" Kyra asked as quietly as possible. "Do you think you're bleeding?"

"Not anymore. I think that place on my stomach stopped bleeding. But I'm so scared."

"I am, too," Kyra admitted. "I know God is here with us, though, and will be with us no matter what."

Gary looked back at them briefly, then faced the front of the van again and turned up the radio. It was on some kind of heavy-metal station that grated on Kyra's nerves. The music sounded harsh, but at least it might offer them the chance to keep talking if they could hear each other over the music.

Before they could have much meaningful conversation, the van pulled off the main road and onto what felt like a gravel road or a trail of some kind. The vehicle came to a stop and Gary got out. Kyra heard a noise she couldn't identify, and then Gary was back in the van. They drove a little farther and the whole routine happened again. Kyra tried to figure out what she had heard, and after a minute it came to her. The noise and Gary's pattern of getting in and out of the van suggested that he was opening gates and driving through them. They were probably on some kind of farm or ranch property.

Her suspicions were confirmed when Gary stopped the vehicle one more time, turning off the ignition. At the passenger side of the van she could see the weathered wood of a building that might be a barn. This time Gary got out and took a few minutes, and Kyra could hear a screeching like unoiled metal on metal. Then Gary came back and jerked the back door of the van open. "Okay, we're going to go inside." He pulled Jasmine roughly to the edge of the hatch and hauled her into a sitting position. She whined softly, but Kyra was sure nobody was going to hear them out here.

As Gary yanked Jasmine to her feet, she stumbled and Kyra gasped. "Don't think you're going to do something heroic," Gary warned. "There's nobody around for over a mile in any direction, so they won't hear you if you scream. And if you try to run I'll kill her. I'd rather take my time, but that won't stop me from doing her in if you try to get away."

With his wild eyes and twitchy demeanor, Kyra believed every word Gary said. She prayed silently, frantically, trying to figure out what to do next. She almost wept in frustration for the cell phone that she had left on the seat of her car. But then she had thought she'd be getting out of the car only long enough to cross the street and get Jasmine. There hadn't been any need for the phone. She wondered if anybody would even miss her such a short a time after she had left her office. Allie knew where she was going, and maybe Josh had gotten back by now. Maybe Jasmine's school would start actively looking for her now that she'd been missing without any word from her for several hours.

Gary was back standing in front of the hatch now, and he pushed and pulled Kyra up to a standing position. The plastic cuffs made her wrists burn and sting behind her back, but she had decided not to give him the pleasure of crying out.

"Come on," he said, half guiding and half dragging her into the barn. "We're going to get started."

Whatever that meant, it couldn't be good. Kyra suppressed a shudder and tried to concentrate on the ground ahead of her.

The gate was open. Josh took that as a good sign, given the dilapidated state of the property he could see behind the trees. There were buildings a distance from the "main" road, which was just a little rural two-lane stretch of asphalt with no shoulder to speak of. "How sure are you that this is it?" he asked Diana quietly. In the backseat, the movement of the car had lulled Sarah to sleep.

"Pretty sure. Do you want to drive just a little way up the property and see if we can find Gary's van?" Josh could tell that Diana was still hoping they wouldn't spot her husband's vehicle and he didn't blame her. What a horrible thing it must be to consider your spouse capable of a crime of the magnitude they had been talking about. He drove slowly up the gravel road at hardly more than a crawl. After the path jogged to the left slightly, he could see what looked like a light-colored van on the side of a weathered gray building.

"That's it," Diana said. She managed to pack all the intensity of a shout into her short, quiet statement. Josh stopped the car, then backed it up until he came to a place where the gravel was a little wider. He turned the car around slowly, trying to avoid the sound of crunching gravel. He drove back to the main road and pulled off into what little flat space was available, about half a mile from the abandoned farmstead. He could see anything that went on outside here, but they were far enough away not to attract immediate attention from anybody in the barn.

Pulling out his cell phone, Josh punched in the numbers for the state police dispatcher that he'd been communicating with most of the afternoon. He delivered a brief message about where they were, and what the situation was, and she promised to send the officers standing by less than five miles away.

He put the phone back in his pocket only to have it vibrate to life almost as soon as he'd let go of it. Allie answered and launched into such quick speech he could hardly follow her. "They found Kyra's truck and her keys only a couple of blocks from Jasmine's school. Her purse was on the floor of the truck, and her phone was on the console."

"Slow down a little. Where were the keys?"

He could hear Allie sigh. "On the street across from

the truck, dropped at the curb and hidden under some trash. I guess we got lucky, because if they'd been out in plain sight I don't think we would have found those keys or the truck they go with."

"You're probably right. Did they find anything else?" Josh didn't want to come straight out and ask about other signs of a struggle, like bullet casings or blood. He nearly sagged in relief when Allie told him that there wasn't anything else besides the keys and truck.

"Wait a minute. There was one more thing, but nobody knows whether it even has any bearing on the disappearance. Under a bus stop bench nearby there was a hardcover book, open on the pavement."

Allie described it a little more. "That's Jasmine's. She had it with her Friday when Kyra picked her up. It should mean that all three of them are together. And I think we've found them."

"Have you called for backup?"

"They're on their way," Josh assured her. "I'll call you back when I have good news." He ended the call to Allie's protests and ignored the phone when it almost immediately started vibrating again.

He knew he should wait for his backup, especially so that he could be sure that Diana and Sarah were safe and stayed at least this far from the barn. But Josh wanted to charge in now just to know that Jasmine and Kyra were unharmed. He strained to hear anything, hoping for raised voices, perhaps, but no screams or gunfire. After about two more minutes he couldn't stand it anymore.

"I need a promise from you that you'll stay right here and make sure Sarah doesn't get out of the car. I don't want to wait any longer out here when I could be doing something to break things up in there. I'm afraid if I wait, somebody's going to get hurt or killed. If we move fast, that might not happen."

Diana looked back at her sleeping child. "Go. We'll stay here. If all three of them are still safe, see if you can keep it that way."

"I will." Josh took his gun out of its shoulder holster and made sure he was ready for anything that might happen. He holstered the gun and walked toward the barn, keeping the closed doors in his focus, moving as quietly as possible and listening for any noise that might be able to tell him how this would all turn out.

FOURTEEN

Kyra strained to see what Gary was doing in the dim light that filtered through the closed door of the barn. Cobwebs and dust didn't make it any easier to discern his expression, and the tears that kept overwhelming her didn't help, either. Mostly he paced and muttered to himself, seemingly trying to decide what to do now and how to do it.

It was much easier to see Jasmine, sitting on the cracked concrete floor of the barn, arms behind her like Kyra's were, stretched uncomfortably and tethered with the plastic handcuffs. Kyra was glad to see that the cut on Jasmine's stomach had stopped bleeding quickly. So far she didn't appear to be in active labor and Kyra prayed that she stayed that way. She could only imagine what Gary would do if Jasmine's water broke or she showed any signs of being in labor. Kyra wasn't sure why, but she thought that something like that would probably send Gary over the edge.

"This is all your fault," Gary said, wheeling around and coming to face Kyra. He loomed over her, standing while she sat on the ground. "You should have just left everything the way it was. There was no reason to disturb anything."

"The floods disturbed everything," Kyra told him. She echoed his language, noticing that he didn't refer to his victims as human beings or even bodies, but just talked about the situation in general. "Once somebody discovered what turned up in the spring floods, I didn't have a choice but to try to identify what had been found."

"You didn't have to try so hard. Nobody missed any of them, really. They were expendable, just like this one." He pointed toward Jasmine.

"Jasmine is not expendable and neither is any other human being. We're all God's creations, and God cares about each of us." Kyra tried to soften the anger in her voice. It wouldn't help their predicament any if she got Gary more upset than he already was. "God cares about you, Gary."

"That's impossible," he said, cutting her off. "Nobody cares about me and they never have. Nobody but Mama ever cared for me. When our house burned down and my folks died, she took me in and raised me. She was the only one who ever told me the fire wasn't my fault. Now she's gone and the demons are back."

He was pacing again, reminding Kyra of an elderly lion in the zoo. "Stop staring at me," he yelled, turning around to face Jasmine. "Why do you have to keep staring?"

Jasmine looked down at the ground, and Kyra could

see that she was terrified. "I wasn't staring. I wasn't even looking. I want to go home."

"Yeah, well so do I, but it's too late for that. None of us are going home again. When I finish, you two will stay here with the others and I'll be going someplace else. Your friend here," he said, pointing to Kyra, "messed things up enough that I can't go home to my family."

Kyra strained at the handcuffs, trying to stretch them just enough to slip one wrist out of the restraints. But they were made of very tough plastic, and she could feel the skin on her arms abrading without any success in freeing herself. "What you did is keeping you away from your family, Gary. But it doesn't have to keep you away forever. You could decide to let us go. If the police aren't outside already they will be soon."

"Then I guess I'd better hurry up here. I want to be long gone before they get here. It's too late to let you go. Besides, I want you to suffer for what you did to me."

Kyra took a deep breath, praying that she would be given the right words to turn their situation around. "Jasmine hasn't done anything to you, Gary. Why don't you let her go? She's pregnant and she isn't well. She won't get far enough to put anybody on your trail by the time you leave here. What do you say?"

"I say you're wasting my time." Gary walked across the open space to a corner and pulled out a duffel bag. Methodically he took several items out of it, including a towel and a large camping flashlight and one other thing that made Kyra's blood chill. He took out a silvery coil of heavy wire and unrolled it slowly between his hands. It stretched out between his hands, the end coiling around one wrist like a snake. Kyra was shaking with fear in the damp barn now, trying to hide the depth of her feelings from this sad, sick man who had claimed so much power over their bodies.

Was this what it felt like to contemplate death? She knew there was something more than this life, and that plenty of good things were waiting for her in heaven. When she thought about it, she always pictured Gran and Lissa Rose there, maybe even together. But she wasn't particularly ready to go today. If she did, she'd never straighten things out between her and Josh, at least not this side of heaven. And here in this awful situation one of the other things she knew was that she wanted to straighten things out with Josh.

She wanted to tell him how much she cared for him, even if that meant that she'd have to listen to him admit that he didn't feel the same way. There was so much more to learn about him, like what he intended to do now that he was going back to the FBI, and how his life was going to be different now that he'd let Jesus into it. She felt a little cheated that she wasn't going to get to know any of that, thanks to Gary.

He was doing something with that wire again, twisting it and turning it between his hands while he murmured to himself too softly for her to understand. Behind him the huge barn door moved a little on its track, and Kyra thought she saw a hand curl around the door at the opening, helping it open just a bit more. If the metal of the track and the rollers at the top grated, Gary would see that someone was coming in.

On impulse Kyra began to scream, loudly enough that it hurt her throat, but it served a dual purpose. Gary paid attention to her, and any noise made by the door sliding open was covered. Jasmine grew wide-eyed, watching her, and Kyra tried to signal her without words to indicate what she was doing. Jasmine's gaze flickered between Kyra and Gary. She must have seen the figure opening the door, because for a moment there was a look of hope instead of panic, and then she joined Kyra in screaming.

"Shut up, both of you. I told you we're miles from anything. Nobody's going to hear you and you're just making my head hurt. You don't want to get me upset." He flexed the wire between his hands and moved toward Jasmine. The tone of her screaming rose higher as he came closer.

The barn door lurched open and Josh stood there, steadying himself and pulling an automatic pistol out of its holster. "Stop now, Griffith. Don't move."

Kyra could have told Josh that threats and orders wouldn't work anymore with Gary. He moved quicker than she thought possible, putting Jasmine between him and Josh as he pulled the wire around her neck fast enough that her scream ended in a gag.

"I won't move as long as you stay where you are," Gary said with a sneer. "Move closer and I'll kill her in twenty seconds. If I pull this taut I can slice her throat so fast you wouldn't have time to fire that thing."

Josh lowered his gun slightly and froze. "Don't do anything more that you'll regret, man. We can all still get out of here alive if nothing else happens. You don't want your wife and daughter to see your picture on the evening news, do you?"

That seemed to stop him for a moment, and Kyra could see the wire slack a little as he loosened his grip. He started to say something, but before he got a word out, noise erupted outside. There was the growl of vehicles, crunching gravel and slamming doors. "Griffith, you're surrounded. Send your hostages out first and throw your weapons out the door. Then come out slowly and nobody gets hurt."

"Don't let them get to you," Josh said, sidestepping to put himself between the open doorway and Jasmine with Gary behind her. "You can let these two go and then you and I will walk out together, okay? Nobody gets hurt, the cops get what they want and we all get out alive."

"Sure. That will happen." Gary's voice held defeat, but Kyra could see that he was still listening to Josh. For the first time in many hours hope rose within her.

Josh stared at the scene before him, trying to think fast enough to gain control before Griffith harmed Jasmine or Kyra. For a tense moment before he'd entered the barn he was afraid that he was too late. Then he realized that Kyra was screaming to create a diversion, not because Griffith was attacking her or the teen. He knew she was resourceful, and that she'd probably risk her own life to save Jasmine if she thought she needed to.

He gave silent thanks when he saw that Griffith didn't appear to have a knife or gun in his hand. The wire garrote was too close to Jasmine for comfort, and Josh knew that, if pressed, Griffith would do what he'd threatened. He suspected that this was the way the other victims had died. It would have been quiet and quick, and the bones that showed up years later would have borne no indication of what went on. Knowing that Griffith's victims probably went quickly wasn't a whole lot of comfort to him. Right now he wanted to make sure there were no more victims, especially not the woman he loved.

He wanted to run to the barn door and scream at whoever was in charge of the operation outside to back off and not press Griffith. He was unstable enough to begin with and they were just making things worse. Normally he didn't share the enmity that a lot of the bureau personnel had for state and local forces, but today he knew how that kind of stuff got started.

"Maybe I'm ready to die. Did you ever think of that?" Griffith challenged him, keeping the wire in his hands. "Maybe having one of those guys out there shoot me, nice and clean, is better than anything else that could happen. And if I kill either of these two that will happen." He gave a humorless laugh.

"If I kill one of them, or even just hurt them badly, I imagine you'll kill me yourself, before the others out there can get to it. Is that right?"

"It could be. But I don't want to have anybody else hurt today, whether it's you or Jasmine or Kyra or even me. And I think you'd really regret dying today in some kind of battle with those guys. Think about Diana and Sarah. Even if you're ready to go, don't they deserve better than to carry that image the rest of their lives?"

Gary appeared to be wavering. The wire was only in one hand now and his words may have been tough, but they came out hesitantly. "Maybe they wouldn't ever see what goes down. Besides, Sarah's just a little kid. She'll never know what is happening. Her mom will see to that."

"Her mom might not have any choice. They're out there, Gary, less than a mile from here. Any ambulance or morgue vehicle that gets in here or leaves will have to pass right by them."

Gary's shoulders drooped. Josh felt as if he almost had him. Then something sailed through the open door and thumped to the floor inside. "That is not a bomb or any kind of incendiary device," a voice called from a bullhorn outside. "We just want to talk."

The package looked like a cell phone wrapped in layers of bubble wrap to cushion its fall. It lay on the barn floor between Josh and Gary. After a few moments it started ringing and vibrating, making the package seem alive.

"You. Pick it up," Gary directed Josh. "Make sure they get the full picture. Tell 'em I'm not coming out now and I'm not sending anybody else out until I talk to Diana and she tells me that she and Sarah are away from here."

"Okay." Josh walked slowly to the package and picked it up. He'd moved about ten feet closer to Gary in the process and he didn't move away once he had the phone. Gary either didn't notice or didn't care.

"This is Special Agent Joshua Richards. Who am I speaking to?"

There was a brief pause. "All you need to know is that I'm the one in charge of at least twenty state troopers ready to blow Griffith's head off. If you'll move out of my SWAT team's sight line we could do just that."

"I'm afraid not, Commander," Josh told him. "Mr. Griffith has a length of piano wire around the throat of one of his hostages and he'll use it. Even a reflex movement would be deadly. He's prepared to agree to your demands if you can have his wife call him and assure him that she and his daughter are in a remote location where they won't be able to witness any arrest or its…aftermath."

"You know I can't do that. Tell Griffith that he's got two minutes to start sending people out or we start sending in tear gas canisters. Hope you don't have any breathing problems, Agent Richards." The phone went dead and Joshua felt like throwing it in frustration.

"Well? I told you nothing good was going to happen, didn't I?" Gary pulled nervously at the wire, which he grasped in both hands again. "What did he say?"

"Not much. And he said he couldn't meet your one demand about Diana and Sarah. I've got a bad feeling about that."

"Yeah, well, I've got a bad feeling about pretty much everything. What's left of my life is going to be ugly." Griffith looked down at the wire in his hands.

Josh knew he had to do something soon or Jasmine might die. In fact, if he wasn't fast enough she and Kyra could both be in danger. It took only seconds for someone to kill another human being with wire and a little hand strength. Even though he kept himself range-qualified all the time, Josh wasn't sure enough of his shooting skills to be able to make the right shot in conditions like this.

What am I supposed to do? He asked in silent distress. It was probably a sin to be this angry with God for letting this whole thing happen this way. He could try to rush Griffith and overpower him, but not without huge risk to Jasmine.

Before he could do anything else, the voice on the bullhorn blared again. "Griffith? Your time is up. Thirty seconds and we throw in the tear gas." It didn't feel like anywhere near that long before a canister was lobbed through the door opening. Above them in the loft of the barn, Josh heard a soft thud that must have been another container. In quick succession he heard two other sounds that made his entire body freeze in shock. The first was a whoosh from the barn loft that mixed the sharp smell of smoke with the acrid scent of the tear gas, and the second was even worse. From the darkened far corner of the barn came a high wail. "Daddy, Daddy, Daddy!" He didn't know how, but somehow Sarah had gotten into the barn.

In that moment everything changed. Josh used Griffith's momentary shock to charge him, pushing his shoulder into the man like a battering man and driving him backward. A shriek from Jasmine stopped his motion and he dropped to his knees between her and Griffith.

"Hold on, Jasmine. You're going to be okay." Josh groped in his pocket to find his small pocket knife and open the blade. As quickly as possible he cut the plastic restraint holding her wrists together and moved her away from the pole.

"It hurts. It hurts so bad." With her freed hand she clutched her throat where the wire had made a small cut.

The tear gas and the smoke were threatening to overwhelm him, but Josh tried to focus on Jasmine instead. Improvising, he helped her pull off her jacket and press it to the two-inch cut on her neck. "It didn't hit a big vein, but we need to get you out there where they can take care of you before you pass out or anything. Can you walk?"

She tried to rise, but shock and stiffness made it a difficult effort. Josh scooped up her long-legged body and mostly carried her through the barn to where the lighter space of the open door stood across the building. "Put the edge of your jacket over your mouth and nose until you get outside," he told her. She nodded in understanding, coughing from the fumes.

"Hostage coming out," Josh yelled as loudly as he could while fighting the smoke and gas. "Get her to an ambulance." All his body wanted to do was stand in the doorway, gulping the cool, sweet air. But Kyra was still back in the barn along with Griffith and Sarah.

He plunged back into the barn, expecting that some of the troopers would follow him by now. But he couldn't see anyone in the smoky atmosphere besides Griffith, stumbling in the far corner of the barn. "Sarah? Where are you, baby? What are you doing here?"

"Daddy?" Her call was followed by deep coughing. "I can't find you."

Josh heard other coughing and used it to locate Kyra. "Keep your arms still while I get you loose," he told her, fumbling again for his pocketknife. He kept his hand between her skin and the blade so that if he slipped he wouldn't cut her. "There. Can you find your way to the door?"

"I think so." He helped her up, catching her when she stumbled. Once she righted herself, he made sure she was going toward the door, then he headed toward the corner where he could hear Griffith choking. Almost all the way to him, Josh felt something on the barn floor and knelt down. Under his fingers was the soft texture of a child's hair.

"Griffith. Over here," he called as he picked up Sarah's limp body. Gary struggled over to them and took Sarah from his arms. "Come on. We'll go out there together. This is what Sarah will remember...her father bringing her to safety."

Now Josh's eyes stung from the tear gas and smoke, but also from memories of the worst night in his own childhood. He realized that somehow he'd been given the gift to keep another child from that kind of trauma. Shoulder to shoulder he pushed through the doorway with Griffith and went outside. "We're coming out and we've got Sarah."

FIFTEEN

"I don't need to be checked over," Kyra said, sitting on the edge of a gurney. "Just get Jasmine to the hospital and send somebody out to look at Sarah and maybe Agent Richards."

"He's refusing attention, too," the paramedic told her. "I think he should be in the ambulance with the young lady, but he sees it differently."

"Probably because he's not going to let go of that child until either her mother or a doctor takes her," Kyra told the paramedic as she watched Josh across the clearing. When he and Gary had come out of the barn together, she noticed that he'd stayed close enough to the other man that there wasn't any chance of anybody taking a shot at either of them. When the troopers rushed them, Gary turned to Josh and handed his daughter to him.

"Take care of her," she heard Gary tell Josh. Then Gary turned back to the troopers who surrounded them and held out his arms to the closest one. "I'll do anything you tell me. Just remember that this is my daughter watching."

Kyra wanted to shout at that moment that he should have remembered his daughter before he abducted someone else's child, before he committed the terrible things that she was sure he had done. But then she saw the moment for what it was; a short, clear moment of sanity for a deeply troubled man. His illness didn't excuse the murders or make him less responsible for them, because Kyra had known other disturbed individuals who didn't harm others.

Apparently Gary's statement had some small effect on the troopers because they quietly handcuffed him, read him his rights, and two officers drove away quickly with him in the back of a car. Now, maybe fifteen minutes later, Josh still held Sarah, who clung to him until another unit pulled up and her mother nearly leaped out of the car. Diana seemed to be using every ounce of self-control she possessed to hold herself back from being hysterical.

"Where did you go? Why did you slip away from me?" she asked Sarah, who just shook her head and buried her face in her mother's shoulder as Josh released her. Once the child was in her mother's arms, she allowed an EMT from a second unit to check her out. While that was happening, Kyra stood up off the gurney in order to go over and talk to Josh, but she didn't get far.

She had enough medical experience to recognize the cold shudders she felt and the light-headedness that suddenly overwhelmed her. The heavy events of the day had her on the edge of shock. Fortunately the paramedic who had tried to convince her to go to the hospital must have suspected what would happen when she stood up, because he was only a step behind her.

"We've still got room on the rig with your friend," he told her, easing her back onto the gurney. "This time I'm not taking no for an answer."

Kyra was too busy listening to the ringing in her ears and willing herself not to pass out to argue with him. On the trip to the hospital she kept floating in and out of full consciousness, aware of the ambulance rocking slightly as it traveled at high speed. The crew member there in the cabin with her and Jasmine checked on her once in a while, but gave most of her attention to Jasmine. That was okay with Kyra because she'd seen the girl's bleeding neck wound and knew she needed a lot more care. Once they got to the hospital she and Jasmine went separate ways. Kyra tried to stay alert enough to ask about how Jasmine was doing, but somewhere in the flurry of activity around her, with oxygen to help her breathe and an IV getting her fluid volume up, Kyra felt that floating sensation again, and this time she didn't fight it.

When she finally woke up feeling more clearheaded, Kyra was surprised to see Allie sitting by her bed. "Hey," her assistant said with a slight smile. "Are you really back this time? You look a little different than you did the couple times you woke up during the night."

Kyra groaned. Somewhere along the line they'd traded the oxygen mask for a cannula, and the clip that held the tubing to her nose pinched slightly. She looked up and found the bag of Ringer's solution she expected attached to an IV in her left hand. "Don't try to talk if your throat hurts," Allie told her. "The doctor said that after being in that place as long as you were with smoke and fumes you'll probably hurt for a day or two."

"Jasmine? And Josh?" she rasped, wincing at the gravelly sound of her voice and the pain saying those few words caused.

"They're both okay," Allie assured her. "Jasmine's just down the hall, and I think later today you'll probably be well enough to go and see her. Josh is all right, too, and he should be discharged today. Maybe after that the two of you can see each other."

Assuming he wants to see me, Kyra thought. He'd been so distant since he heard about Lissa Rose that she wasn't sure that he would want to have much to do with her.

"Do you want me to check with the nurses to see when you can go see Jasmine?"

"Yes," Kyra said, surprised at how much effort it took to stay alert and hold a conversation. Allie left the room and Kyra drifted off into a light doze again. Several times during the morning a nurse or doctor came in and most of her needles and other annoyances were removed.

Her throat felt sore, but she no longer needed any supplemental oxygen. The IV was removed, and the doctor placed a large foam pitcher in front of her that contained ice water. "I'll make this trade if you'll be sure to drink plenty of water. If you don't do that, then we'll have to go back to the needles."

"I'll do it," Kyra told him, trying not to wince as she spoke to him, and swallowed some of the contents of her cup.

"Good. If you keep doing things right we can let you go tomorrow," he told Kyra. "Between now and then you need to start getting up and walking around the halls some. We'll make sure you have a second gown so that you avoid any embarrassing situations. I understand you want to visit another patient, anyway. And she's indicated she wants to see you, so there's no problem there."

"Jasmine," Kyra said. "How is she?"

"An inch or two in the wrong direction and she wouldn't have made it. We're monitoring her to make sure she doesn't show any signs of going into labor, but so far so good."

Kyra sagged back against the pillows in relief. "Good. Can I have that gown now?"

"Soon," he promised. "I'll instruct your nurse to bring it to you as soon as she sees that you've had at least another pint of fluids. And maybe a late breakfast of something soft and easy to swallow, okay?"

Kyra nodded and found herself smiling. This was about the best possible outcome in an awful situation. She'd been praying nearly constantly, prayers of thanks and gratitude every time she thought of something else that could have gone terribly wrong, but didn't. Now she settled in on the pillows and just praised God for all of it, the good and the bad, while the hospital noises hummed around her and she sipped her cool water. She was ready to go see Jasmine, and the sooner she followed all the doctor's conditions, the sooner she'd get there.

Josh sat at Jasmine's bedside, marveling at how good she looked despite what she'd been through. "You can say otherwise all you want, but you saved my life, Mr. Richards. Mine and Miss Kyra's and probably even…his." Josh understood her reluctance to say Griffith's name. "I'm not sure you should have done that for him. He was going to kill all of us."

"He might have," Josh admitted. "But once I knew that Sarah was there I wasn't about to hurt her father in front of her. Jasmine, I spent more than twenty years trying to get over my own dad's death and prove he was a hero and not the loser everybody else said he was. It ate up my life, and I wasn't about to give somebody else that kind of nightmare."

"Wow. It would be harder for her, too, because I don't know if there's that much good to prove about her dad, huh?" Once again Josh was struck with the insight this kid showed.

"Have you thought any about what you're going to do with your life, kid? Because you sound to me like somebody who'd make a good psychologist or detective. Sometimes there's not that much difference between the two."

Jasmine shook her head. "Not me. My grades aren't that good and now I'll have a baby to look after. I figure that pretty much finishes my school career."

Josh reached out and took her hand. "It better not. Do you want your son or daughter to get the message that it's okay to throw away your gifts because life gets hard?"

"No. But how could I ever manage a baby and school? I'll have to work to support us and find a place to live when I age out of the system."

"I expect there are people who would be willing to help, me included." Josh didn't even surprise himself with his statement. He'd been single for so long, with relatively simple needs that he had a decent amount of savings. "And there's one other hard question that I suspect people have been asking you to consider."

He didn't even have to spell things out. "Right. Whether or not I should keep this baby. One of the social workers has probably told me about two dozen times that I should give him or her up for adoption right away. That I owe the baby that much, to be raised in a stable two-parent home where they have plenty of money and all that."

"What do you think?" Josh watched her thin shoulders slump.

"I don't know. Sometimes I think she's right. If I'd had all that I probably wouldn't be in the system. But then I look at kids like Ashley. She started out in one of those 'good homes' with two parents and everything, but then her folks split up and her mom got in a car accident and she's in the same mess I am."

"You don't have to decide alone." The raspy voice from the doorway made Josh and Jasmine both turn to see who was talking. It was Kyra, looking a little pale and leaning on the door frame for support. Her hair was wild and she wore two mismatched hospital gowns, one front to back, and hospital-issue slipper socks.

Josh stood quickly and pointed her to the chair he'd just vacated. "Sit down before you fall down. You still look pretty peaked."

"Yeah, you can blame some of that on my English and Irish ancestors. Pale redheads look extra-pale when they're sick."

"I think you probably make me look healthy," Jasmine cracked, grinning slightly. "Mr. Richards is right, Miss Kyra. You look like you might pass out again."

"Well, I don't feel that bad," she said, a little snappish. Josh noticed she sat down, anyway, and her coloring improved slightly once she settled into the chair. "In fact, they're telling me that if I keep doing everything they tell me I'll be out of here tomorrow. Looks like somebody else is ready to go now."

Josh felt like sitting down again to regain his balance when her green eyes surveyed him. "The doctor would have been happier if I'd stayed another day, but I hate these places. And I promised to do everything he said. Now that your part of the case is done, or at least in no more need of an investigator, it's time for me to clear out."

"Is the bureau ready to take you back?"

She always cut straight to the point. It was one of the things he liked most about Kyra. "I talked to my supervisor this morning and she said yes. I told her I've got a couple of personal things to wrap up and then I'd see her in Virginia."

"Any way I can help with those personal things?" Kyra asked. He wasn't sure why she looked a little unhappy with what he said. Maybe she was afraid that he would stick her with all the paperwork for the case. Or maybe she wasn't as resentful of him as Josh thought she'd be.

He cleared his throat before he answered, Kyra's painful-sounding voice making him aware of his own discomfort. "Not much," he told her. "Most of it I'm still working out for myself."

"Okay. If you need somebody to bounce ideas off of, you know where to find me." He reached down and took Jasmine's hand again briefly and gave it a quick squeeze. The action allowed him to keep his face out of Kyra's line of vision so she wouldn't see the tears springing up in his eyes. He could have talked to the two of them for hours, but he knew that wasn't what he needed to do.

When he straightened back up, Kyra rose from the chair. "Thank you," she said, putting her arms around him for a heartfelt hug. "I heard what Jasmine said earlier and she's right. You probably saved both of our lives."

"I should have done more. I could have been quicker," Josh blurted out. "I thought you'd be angry at me for not getting to you sooner once I found you."

Her eyes widened in surprise. From the little distance between them, Josh saw golden flecks in the green. "You're kidding. I thought you were wonderful. And you've been hiding some real talents as a negotiator."

He let go reluctantly of her warm body and stepped back, fighting the urge to kiss her instead for the gift her words gave him. "Maybe. And thank you. Just hearing the way you feel makes me feel better." He straightened his shoulders, ready to leave the room while he still had the courage to do it. "Any messages you want me to deliver at work while I clear my stuff out?"

She shook her head. "Tell them I'll probably be in Friday for a little while, but not to expect much out of me."

"I guess not. Take care of yourself. And you, too, Jasmine."

"We will," Kyra said softly. "And we'll take care of each other." The last sight Josh had of them was their hands meeting across the white sheet, fingers linking in comfort and love.

"This is Pam Gorman. What did you do to my best agent?" Kyra didn't automatically recognize the irritated voice on the other end of the phone, but she looked at the caller ID and saw a number she recognized as FBI from the area code and prefix.

"What do you mean? Josh said he was going back to the bureau last week."

There was a harrumph from the phone. "He came back, all right. Just long enough to resign his position and clean out his desk. He told me he was taking a transfer to something that suited him better. What did you do, entice him over there permanently?"

"Not at all. In fact, I was about ready to call there

and see what he was up to," Kyra admitted. She didn't go on to tell Pam that Josh hadn't called, e-mailed or written since he'd left Jasmine's hospital room, and she was getting concerned. The less she said, the less likely it was that she'd betray the feelings Josh had stirred up in her.

Pam sighed. "Well, why don't we agree to contact each other if we hear from him, okay? I sent you a man one step from a spectacular burnout and got back an individual who looked calm and in control. Too bad he only stuck around a couple of hours."

"Yes," Kyra agreed. "I'll call you if I hear anything."

"The same goes here." There was a short pause on Pam's end of the phone. "You're not set up to be a training school, are you? Because I've got a couple of other agents who could use some of what Josh apparently picked up."

Kyra stifled a short laugh. "Sorry, that was a one-shot deal. Have a good day, Ms. Gorman."

Kyra spent the rest of the morning wondering where Josh might have gotten to. Once she came back to work Friday his part of the office was neat and empty. The laptop sat closed on her desk and everything pertaining to his work on the case was typed up and placed in a file folder along with his notes and other information. Nothing about the office hinted that two people had shared it for a number of weeks. Even now it felt a bit empty.

Kyra found herself absently running one fingertip around the corner of the laptop when she had an idea.

She opened the laptop and turned it on, hoping that Josh hadn't done his searching on a computer at home. She traced back through sites he'd visited and a few he'd even bookmarked. Half an hour later she had the information she wanted. She held the piece of paper with the phone number she'd printed out, wondering if she should make a call or not. If she was wrong, it might cause a bit of a problem for Josh. Even if she were right he might not want her to find him.

Looking down at the number again, she decided to pray about it for the rest of the day and listen to see if God's answer for her got any clearer. Right now what she thought about doing sounded as much her idea as it might be God's. If the balance tipped a little in God's favor, she'd make the phone call.

Wednesday morning, Ranger sat on one of the chair cushions in the kitchen, watching Kyra pace across the room. She must have been irritating him with her constant movement, because he took a swipe at the edge of her sweater the next time she got close to him. "I know, kitty. I should sit down, but I can't right now." She'd picked up one of the cordless phones three times now, punched in part of a number in Iowa and put it back down.

She looked at the clock again. Nine-fifteen, which meant that in Davenport it must be eight-fifteen. "That's not too early for somebody with grade-school-aged kids, is it?" she mused, laughing when the cat talked back with a sound that surely sounded like a "no."

"I'll take your advice," she told him, finally punching in the entire number and sitting down at the table, holding her breath while the phone rang. Before she could hang up, a woman answered with a soft "Hello?"

"Hi. May I speak to Chrissie?"

"This is Chris. Nobody calls me Chrissie except—" she faltered "—except my brother. Are you looking for him?"

"I am. My name is Kyra Elliott and—"

"You don't have to say anything else. I've heard a lot about you in the past three days. I keep telling Josh he's crazy not to call you, but he's as stubborn as he was when he was twelve. He's not here yet so I can say that out loud." The woman gave a short laugh. "Once he gets back from taking the girls to school I'll have to be quieter, won't I?"

"Probably not. I don't plan to talk all that long. I was just anxious to see if he'd found you, and if the two of you had gotten together."

"We have, and I think I should thank you for that. I've never seen my brother act the way he has the past three days. Of course, there was a long time when I didn't see him at all. I'm glad we're talking again. My kids don't have any other aunts or uncles, and it was beginning to feel wrong not to have any contact with the one they do have. And once I didn't talk to Josh after he sent me all the stuff on our father, I never expected he'd make the first move to get in touch."

"Has he said anything about quitting his job?" Kyra

knew it probably wasn't any of her business, but she wanted to know if Josh would ever be coming back here close enough that they might develop a relationship.

"He said he didn't quit exactly, he's transferring to another job. But first he has to take this course in negotiations and conflict. He says he's already signed up for the next one they're giving at Quantico."

All the pieces of the puzzle fell into place for Kyra then and she had to fight tears. "Wow. He really did take my advice."

"Was that your advice, too? Now I really think he should get back there and start courting you."

Kyra could hear all kinds of noise in the background on Chrissie Morgan's end of the phone; doors opening and closing and a small voice talking excitedly about doughnut holes and the high-pitched yap of a dog barking. "Josh, I hope you didn't get him the chocolate kind. If he drops one it will make Gizmo sick. Okay, good. Here, talk to your girlfriend while I get Timothy some milk to go with those."

Before Kyra could protest or hang up, she could hear the phone change hands and the background noise grow fainter. "I didn't tell anybody I was your girlfriend," she protested. "Chrissie decided that on her own."

"My kid sister's good at that. But I have to admit that she's grown up into a very astute woman. She's been telling me all week that I ought to make sure you *are* my girlfriend. What do you think?"

"I think it sounds like a great idea, provided you're coming back. I don't do long distance very well."

"I don't think I would, either, Kyra. Which is why I took a big leap of faith and applied for the bureau's resident agency in Baltimore."

"As a hostage negotiator?"

"We're called crisis negotiators, thank you. And I won't be official until I go through the course the first two weeks of June. After that, assuming I pass—"

"Which you will," Kyra put in.

"Thank you. Assuming I pass, I'll be required to go all kinds of places around the world to help work out hostage situations, kidnappings, anything like that where a U.S. citizen is involved. Is that okay with you?"

"Sure. It sounds like you've found your place."

"In more ways than one. Kyra, my whole life is different since I walked into your office. You've shown me the way to faith, and love and now hope, so I actually have a purpose in life. You said you thought I saved your life. Well, I know you saved mine."

Kyra didn't even bother to fight the tears, mostly happy ones that fell now. "Maybe we saved each other, Josh."

"Maybe we did. But we didn't do it alone. God helped a lot." He paused for a moment and Kyra thought he was getting more serious, but his next words belayed that notion. "Will you meet me at the airport Friday night? I'd talk more, but right now I have to go have a glass of milk and some doughnut holes with my three-year-old nephew, followed by an antihistamine chaser. There's this animal that looks like half a pair of bunny slippers that thinks I'm his new best friend. Love you, Kyra."

"I love you, too, Josh. We can talk later and set up the airport stuff." And Kyra hung up, feeling like waltzing for joy, which she did, using Ranger as a partner. If he thought there was something odd about her humming "Amazing Grace" and dancing him around in her arms, he didn't show it. Instead, he added his rumbling purr to the roar of joy in her heart.

"I'll never be one of the boys again," she whispered into Ranger's furry neck.

This was the beginning of a new life, and she could hardly wait until Friday.

Dear Reader,

I have a tremendous amount of respect for the individuals who protect and serve all of us, and I hope that my stories show that. Several members of my extended family work as nurses, paramedics, firefighters and in law enforcement, and several more are a part of my "church family" as well. I could never do what they do, and I hope that I thank them and others in their fields enough for the tremendous service they provide. I hope that if you've enjoyed Kyra and Josh's story you might take a few minutes and find a way to thank someone you know who works in one of those tough and dangerous professions.

Blessings,

Lynn Bulock

QUESTIONS FOR DISCUSSION

1. Why do you think the author used the verse from Psalm 9 as the theme verse for this book? What other verses might also apply to the story?

2. Have you ever felt abandoned? By God? By friends or family? What made you feel better? What advice would you give to children and teens who have been abandoned?

3. Kyra wishes that her coworkers didn't treat her like "one of the boys." Have you ever been in a similar situation? How did you handle it?

4. At the beginning of the story, Josh feels as if he has nothing to lose. How could he have made better choices?

5. At first Kyra and Josh aren't too thrilled to be working together. How could they have made the situation better? Have you ever had to work with someone you disliked? What did you learn from the experience?

6. Josh and Kyra are trying to find the identities of three murder victims. Why do you think the killer was able to hide his victims' identities for so long? The killer was able to keep up appearances of a

normal life. Do you think someone could do this in real life? How did you feel about the killer's family?

7. Kyra's grandmother was the best person in her life growing up. Who was yours? Was this person also the most influential person in your life? What affected you the most—negative or positive influences? Discuss.

8. Kyra lives her faith by working with at-risk teens. What kinds of things so you do, or would you like to do, to help your community? How does serving your community coincide with your faith?

10. Kyra tells Josh that our culture uses money and power as idols. Do you agree or disagree with her? Why? Discuss examples from popular culture.

11. Kyra gives Josh a copy of *The Message* to read. What kind of bible would you give someone who knew little or nothing about scripture? What else would you do to introduce someone to your faith?

12. Do you think it's harder to rely on God or on people? Why?

13. How do you think it feels to face a life-or-death situation?

REQUEST YOUR FREE BOOKS!
2 FREE RIVETING INSPIRATIONAL NOVELS
PLUS 2 FREE MYSTERY GIFTS

YES! Please send me 2 FREE Love Inspired® Suspense novels and my 2 FREE mystery gifts (gifts are worth about $10). After receiving them, if I don't wish to receive any more books, I can return the shipping statement marked "cancel". If I don't cancel, I will receive 4 brand-new novels every month and be billed just $4.24 per book in the U.S. or $4.74 per book in Canada, plus 25¢ shipping and handling per book and applicable taxes, if any*. That's a savings of over 20% off the cover price! I understand that accepting the 2 free books and gifts places me under no obligation to buy anything. I can always return a shipment and cancel at any time. Even if I never buy another book, the two free books and gifts are mine to keep forever.

123 IDN ERXX   323 IDN ERXM

Name	(PLEASE PRINT)	
Address		Apt. #
City	State/Prov.	Zip/Postal Code

Signature (if under 18, a parent or guardian must sign)

Order online at www.LoveInspiredSuspense.com

Or mail to Steeple Hill Reader Service:

IN U.S.A.: P.O. Box 1867, Buffalo, NY 14240-1867
IN CANADA: P.O. Box 609, Fort Erie, Ontario L2A 5X3

Not valid to current subscribers of Love Inspired Suspense books.

Want to try two free books from another series?
Call 1-800-873-8635 or visit www.morefreebooks.com

* Terms and prices subject to change without notice. N.Y. residents add applicable sales tax. Canadian residents will be charged applicable provincial taxes and GST. Offer not valid in Quebec. This offer is limited to one order per household. All orders subject to approval. Credit or debit balances in a customer's account(s) may be offset by any other outstanding balance owed by or to the customer. Please allow 4 to 6 weeks for delivery. Offer available while quantities last.

Your Privacy: Steeple Hill Books is committed to protecting your privacy. Our Privacy Policy is available online at www.SteepleHill.com or upon request from the Reader Service. From time to time we make our lists of customers available to reputable third parties who may have a product or service of interest to you. If you would prefer we not share your name and address, please check here. ☐

LISUS08R

Love Inspired®
SUSPENSE

TITLES AVAILABLE NEXT MONTH

Don't miss these four stories in August

THE GUARDIAN'S MISSION by Shirlee McCoy
The Sinclair Brothers
Heartbroken after a failed engagement, Martha Gabler
heads to her family's cabin for some time alone. But her
retreat soon turns deadly. With gunrunners threatening
her life, Martha has to trust undercover ATF agent
Tristan Sinclair to protect her—and heal her heart.

HIDDEN DECEPTION by Leann Harris
Elena Segura Jackson is frightened when she stumbles
upon her employee murdered, and she's terrified when
the killer starts vandalizing her shop. Clearly, she has
something the killer wants...but what is it? With Detective
Daniel Stillwater's help, can she find it in time to save
her life?

HER ONLY PROTECTOR by Lisa Mondello
All bounty hunter Gil Waite wants is to find a fugitive and
collect the reward. Then he meets the fugitive's beautiful
sister. Trapped in Colombia while rescuing her brother's
baby, Sonia Montgomery needs Gil on her side if she's ever
going to get herself and her niece safely home.

RIVER OF SECRETS by Lynette Eason
Amy Graham fled to Brazil to atone for her family's sins—
she never expected to discover Micah McKnight, the man
her mother betrayed. Micah doesn't remember who he is,
and Amy is too scared to tell him...but as danger escalates,
Amy's secrets could cost her everything.

LISCNM0708